First published in Great Britain by
HarperCollins Children's Books in 2012
HarperCollins Children's Books is a division of
HarperCollinsPublishers Ltd,
77-85 Fulham Palace Road, Hammersmith, London W6 8JB

The HarperCollins website address is
www.harpercollins.co.uk
1

ISBN-13 978-0-00-743001-7

Printed and bound in England by
Clays Ltd, St Ives plc

THE PEPPERS
AND THE INTERNATIONAL MAGIC GUYS

SIÂN PATTENDEN

Illustrated by Jimmy Pickering

HarperCollins *Children's Books*

The Troupe

Uncle Potty

Maureen

Monty

Esmé

Clive

Bernard

Nigella

Stupeedo

Contents

An excerpt from

Dr Pompkins – Totality Magic

TRICK: Magnetic Sugar Lumps

Tell your friends that sugar lumps are magnetic; as you place a full bowl in front of you, pick up one lump, then "stick" it to another and hold both aloft.

Watch your pals' frustration as they try to do the same!

———

Of course, you prepared a lump beforehand with a small dab of butter, but your friends are not to know that…

The Secrets of the Great Magicians

If you are reading this book then undoubtedly you have a thirst to learn the secrets of the great magicians who perform such tricks regularly. I, Dr Pompkins, famed for tricks including my one-legged straitjacket escape act in a telephone box full of water and 25 man-eating lizards, can teach you some of them.

Read on, dear performer, and you too could be filling audiences with astonishment and joy. If you enjoy magic, and I believe that you must do, then walk beside me on this fantastical journey and we shall see great sights and experience true wonders.

In all totality,

Dr Pompkins

CHAPTER ONE

The "Trick of all Tricks"

Four days ago Uncle Potty had come to stay with eleven-year-old Pepper twins – Esmé and Monty. It was the summer holidays and while Mr and Mrs Pepper went on a quick trip to an ancient woodland site, Uncle Potty was in charge. The best and most exciting thing about this was that Uncle Potty was a professional conjuror, a member of the International Magic Guys (IMG) club, which

happened to be based round the corner from the Peppers' home in Highwood Road. The next best thing, as far as Monty was concerned, was that Uncle Potty was always practising magic and therefore always in need of an assistant. Monty had been delighted to help. He had fetched and carried for Uncle Potty (so far Monty had cleaned fourteen magic tumblers and one plastic bowl), polished Uncle Potty's patent leather shoes and glued his magic top hat back together where it had split.

Uncle Potty was impossibly old and extremely tall. As a consequence, his sleeves reached his elbows and his trouser hems were always by his shins. He found it difficult

to navigate those tiny waistcoat pockets with such long fingers and when he started to become anxious – like now – his hair would stick up on end, looking like crazy woollen worms on a roller-coaster ride. Uncle Potty's eyebrows also seemed to have been knitted – to form one gigantic, fluffy strip. He had a loud voice and a basic theatricality. He could not have been anything other than a magician, although the rest of his family were a roaring success in the dry-cleaning business.

However, as thrilling as it was having a magician in the house, Esmé had begun to notice that most of Uncle Potty's tricks seemed to end in disaster. Worryingly,

Uncle Potty had taken over the kitchen at the Peppers' home all morning and was now standing by the kitchen table, ready to perform his latest act. Uncle Potty had so far removed the items in his way – Esmé's homework notebook, a library book about wildlife, the Peppers' laptop and some sticks that had yet to serve a purpose – and put them on the floor. In their place was a large bowl of water and five different fruits placed in a line – a kiwi, a melon, a medium-sized pineapple, an apple and a tangerine. The fruits were a little squashed and soggy and Uncle Potty had brightly coloured stains all over his shirt.

"I have discovered the trick of all tricks,"

14

announced Potty, long arms in the air. "It involves making a watch disappear, then to be revealed in a piece of… fruit."

Esmé gave Potty an encouraging look, even though the trick sounded quite complicated.

"What's the time, Esmé?" asked Uncle Potty, in a dramatic voice. Esmé glanced at the extremely reliable watch that her mum had given her when she got a high grade in last year's maths test and announced, "Half past twelve."

Esmé waited for Uncle Potty's next line, but instead Monty popped his head up from under the table, where he was supposed to be hiding. He handed Uncle Potty a long strip of paper.

"What's that?" Esmé asked.

"Nothing," said Monty. "You weren't supposed to see."

"Please get back under the table, Monty," said Uncle Potty, politely but firmly. "I have the item now."

Monty reluctantly disappeared again.

"Ahem, thus we have safely concluded that it is half past twelve," announced Uncle Potty. "May I see your watch, Esmé?"

Raising her left wrist, Esmé revealed her treasured Timex. Uncle Potty quickly unsnapped the watch from Esmé's wrist before she could stop him and hid it behind his back. There was a scuffling sound as he handed the watch to Monty.

"Time is an extraordinary thing!" said Uncle Potty, even louder. "It reminds us that the bus is late, it flows with the seasons and it, er, gives us wrinkles."

"Could I have my watch back, please?" Esmé asked, suddenly realising her watch was going to be hidden in a piece of soggy fruit, which might do it more harm than good.

"Of course!" replied Uncle Potty, searching his multi-coloured waistcoat pockets for something.

"Aha, your elegant timepiece!" said Uncle Potty, as he retrieved the now-crinkled strip of paper and balanced it on Esmé's wrist. It had a badly drawn clock face on it,

18

showing the time: 12.30pm.

"This isn't my watch, Uncle, it's a piece of paper," said Esmé. The strip quivered on her hand and then fell off.

"Well observed, young Esmé. So where is your real watch?" Uncle Potty spoke excitedly now. He picked up an apple. "Shall I ask the magic tangerine?"

"That's not a tangerine…" Esmé noted.

"Oh, er, yes." Uncle Potty tried to cover himself. "Just a little joke," he smiled. "I will now dip all the fruit into the bowl of water to show you that your watch is not inside any of them.

"Take this apple for instance," Uncle Potty continued, dunking the apple in the water. "Your watch is not in here! Hurrah!"

There was another scuffling sound and the tangerine started wobbling on the table.

An object fell on the floor with a tiny clang – a broken-watch sort of clang.

"I can't do it!" whispered Monty audibly from under the table. "It won't go in the hole."

Esmé winced. She hoped Uncle Potty was not about to make a big mistake. What was happening to her watch?

"Pick another fruit," Uncle Potty said to Esmé. "Maybe the kiwi?"

Esmé looked blank, but Uncle Potty seized the kiwi anyway and dunked it energetically into the bowl of water.

"No watch in here!" he hollered. "Shall I try the tangerine, finally?"

Esmé looked at the fruit trembling on the tablecloth. She assumed Monty was trying to stuff her watch inside it. But maybe this was a double bluff – her watch was in someone's pocket. Or maybe the trick involved an optical illusion and the water wasn't really water, but something dry. But Esmé feared the worst.

"Could I just have my Timex back, please?" Esmé asked.

"Of course," Uncle Potty replied, picking up the tangerine from which Esmé's watch strap dangled.

"My watch!" said Esmé and made a grab

for the strap before Uncle Potty could submerge it in the water. But as she did so:

Shhhhlooop!

The bowl tipped over and water went everywhere – on to the table, Monty, the laptop on the floor, Esmé's homework, the library book, the sticks…

"My sticks!" said Monty, appearing sodden from under the table.

"Your sticks? Look at my homework! Look at the laptop! Mum and Dad will kill us." Esmé grabbed a tea towel and desperately started mopping water from the laptop, then her homework notebook. "Everything's ruined!" she cried.

Uncle Potty started to tremble.

"Oh, me, oh, my... Monty, find some more teachers, er I mean tea cloths. I'll go and get a sponge. Oh, Esmé, I'm terribly sorry."

Uncle Potty handed Esmé the tangerine, with her watch half-stuffed inside. "I hadn't meant for the bowl of water to be so... full."

Esmé took the fruit-splattered Timex, sticky and dripping, and wiped it with her sleeve. The second hand had definitely stopped; there was no ticking sound. Esmé was crestfallen. It had been a very accurate watch.

"I'll save up and buy you a new one," said Monty, wiping the library book with an old towel. "I'll go out and perform some street magic."

Uncle Potty appeared from the garden with the mop that had a wobbly handle. "Or we could write our own magic book, Monty, and make a fortune!"

"Brilliant!" said Monty. "I'll go and get a pen."

As kind as these offers were, Esmé did not think that they were going to provide an immediate solution to the problems in hand. Things were getting out of control. The living room was becoming cluttered with magic books, the stairs covered in little plastic boxes with false panels and double hinges – and Uncle Potty kept throwing his stage clothes everywhere, ignoring the designated dirty washing bin. Now things

24

were being damaged – Esmé's homework, her watch, the laptop... Was the computer under guarantee? How would the family ever afford a new one? Esmé had been using it to help write a homework assignment about beluga whales on it. It was probably lost for ever. Esmé sighed loudly. She mustn't get too upset. It wasn't really Uncle Potty and Monty's fault – it was Esmé who had actually knocked the water bowl. But Esmé did not think that anything would change until drastic measures were taken.

An excerpt from

Dr Pompkins – Totality Magic

TRICK: The Aerial Ball

A Ping-Pong ball is best for this trick.

The ball is held in one hand, then suddenly glides through the air to the other.

The secret? Thread a piece of black thread through the ball – the forefingers of both hands hold the loop taut, forming a sort of track along which the ball slides. The lightness of the Ping-Pong ball is an asset to this trick, as your friends will see.

———

Just do not let them stand too close to you…

Repetition

The golden rule that any magician knows is never, ever, to repeat a trick to the same audience. Once the element of surprise is missing, the audience – or at least part of it – will work out how the trick is done. It only takes a slight difference from one performance to the next to see the mechanics of the act itself. As I was saying to Mrs Dr Pompkins only yesterday over a nice glass of sherry and a Chelsea bun – repetition is the enemy of surprise.

In all totality,

Dr Pompkins

CHAPTER TWO

Mind Magic

Esmé was small for her age; she was sensible-looking and always wore trousers and flat shoes. Her brother Monty was not an identical twin – his hair was lighter and he had more freckles (and besides, he was a boy). In general, he looked relatively sensible, until yesterday, that is, when they had all gone to the local party shop. Monty had spied a black sateen cape, which he excitedly purchased

with three months' pocket money. From the moment he put it on, Esmé thought, he did not look very sensible at all.

That in itself was not a huge issue. The real issue was that Esmé had been subjected to non-stop magic for the last few days and she was beginning to feel overawed. As Uncle Potty stood mopping in the kitchen, Esmé thought back to the cause of the current trouble: Dr Pompkins.

On the morning that he arrived, exactly four days ago, Uncle Potty gave Monty a book called Dr Pompkins – Totality Magic, as a source of magical inspiration for his new assistant. As soon as he opened the musty pages of the book, Monty was enraptured.

Sitting in the armchair in the living room, he immediately insisted on trying Pompkins out on Esmé. The first thing that he wanted to try, Monty explained, was "a highly simple card trick, in all totality".

"Pick a card, any card," he said, producing a deck that he splayed into an irregular fan shape with his fingers.

Esmé chose the Jack of Hearts, memorised it and put it back into the deck carefully.

"And now, my magic shuffle!" said Monty.

Monty had read something about shuffling the cards in a certain way, which actually meant not shuffling them at all. For a few seconds Monty shifted the cards from one hand to the other, without actually changing the order. He kept a watch on Esmé's card all the way through.

However, eagle-eyed Esmé noticed what he was doing – or rather, what he was *not* doing.

"Are you shuffling properly?" she asked.

"Just keep thinking of your card, Esmé," Monty replied. "Do not forget."

Monty fixed his twin sister with what was supposed to be a hypnotic expression, but which looked closer to someone trying to contain a burp. "Magic is supposed to make people 'suspend their disbelief – to believe things they wouldn't ordinarily believe'. I read that in Dr Pompkins," he said.

"I do believe," replied Esmé. "I believe that

you are not shuffling properly on purpose."

Monty picked – a card from the middle of the deck – it was the Jack of Hearts.

"See!" said Monty. "I just need to take some time to get the technique right, the sleight of hand."

"Yes, maybe that's all it needs," said Esmé, who didn't want to dampen her brother's enthusiasm.

Montague Pepper picked up Dr Pompkins' book and silently started on a new chapter. Esmé carried on with her summer homework assignment, the one which was based around beluga whales and the fact that a scientist in Japan had discovered they could understand five basic words, which included "bucket"

and "goggles". Esmé decided to draw a large picture of a beluga whale, which she did carefully – adding arrows that pointed to parts of the animal, for instance its huge brain, a fin and the bit where she thought the ears might be.

After twenty minutes, Monty set the book down.

"I am now going to perform mind magic on you, Esmé," he said with great seriousness.

"You are in the right frame of mind," he continued. "You have been so absorbed in your work that your brain is emitting what Dr Pompkins calls 'mega waves'."

Although Esmé thought that "mega waves" sounded utterly ridiculous, she did

think that "mind magic" was interesting. She had seen a certain Derek Brown perform this sort of routine on TV and she had been fascinated by how he made ordinary people believe in all kinds of nonsense – from ghosts and spirits to making them think that they could rob a bank or steal a race horse. Esmé liked the idea of hypnosis, but only on other people. Would Monty make her fall into a trance – only to find he was not able to wake her up again? And would he also send himself into a reverie? Esmé could not remember Monty doing anything even vaguely hypnotic before, apart from a very odd dance on Christmas Day last year after he'd eaten a large bowl full of profiteroles.

And if Esmé remembered rightly, Monty had been sick fifteen minutes later.

"Look into my eyes," Monty suddenly commanded. "Go on, really concentrate."

Esmé did what she was told. Maybe this time she would suspend her disbelief. She looked into Monty's left eye, then his right, then back to the left again.

"My eyes are wiggling," she said. "Is that normal?"

The longer Esmé stared, the more her eyes wiggled, and the more she thought about her eyes wiggling the less hypnotised she felt.

Now Monty spoke in a low, long voice: "Your mega waves are definitely vibrating. I want you to draw whatever comes into your mind." He handed Esmé a blank sheet of A4 paper.

"When you've finished, fold the paper once," Monty said, taking his own sheet of paper. "And I, the great Montague Pepper, will draw the exact same thing using my own mega waves that are connecting with yours, miaow."

"Draw *anything*?" asked Esmé.

"Anything, *miaow*," he replied.

Esmé was not sure she'd heard right. "Anything, *miaow*?" she repeated.

"Use your, um, *miaow* imagination," said Monty quickly, under his breath, to drive the point home.

Esmé raised an eyebrow at her brother. Feeling mischievous, she thought it would be funny to draw a small sausage dog. She did so and folded the paper up twice.

"Once, not twice," Monty said, sighing. "Oh, well. Now let us show the powers for enjoined mega waves and open our pictures! 1 – 2 – 3!"

Dramatically, they each opened their drawings.

"A cat!" exclaimed Monty proudly of his picture, before realising that Esmé was holding up a picture of a dog – and what's more, a sausage dog.

Monty looked devastated.

"You didn't draw a cat," he said.

"Er, no," said Esmé. "You kept saying miaow so I thought…"

"…that you'd do the opposite."

"Sorry, Monty," Esmé said, realising that her brother was upset. "I'll try harder next time."

Four days of magic and chaos later and Esmé was standing in the devastated kitchen, wondering just what to do. Some of the plastic floor tiles looked like they were curling up at the edges under all that water, not helped by Uncle Potty's low quality mopping. Uncle Potty heard Esmé sigh again and reached into one of his many waistcoat pockets and brought out a bunch of silk flowers.

"To cheer you up," he said. Esmé tried to smile, but the corners of her mouth were not having any of it.

Uncle Potty reached into another pocket with some difficulty and found a sweetie tube that contained a selection of nuts and bolts. He put it back and then found a five-pound note from another pocket. His waistcoat certainly had a lot of potential.

"Here, Esmé. I know I can't replace everything, but you could at least get yourself some chocolate from the CostSnippas convenience store," said Uncle Potty kindly. "Maybe even a new pencil from the stationery shelf."

"And a homework book as well?" asked Esmé.

"Why not?" said Uncle Potty. "Monty and I will finish clearing up here while you're away and everything will be shipshape when you come back."

"OK, thanks," said Esmé, reaching for her coat.

As she went for the front door, Esmé heard her brother say, "I've got a new trick, Uncle Potty," he said. "What about turning a pineapple into a bicycle?"

Esmé sighed as she stepped out of the door and closed it quietly behind her.

An excerpt from

Dr Pompkins – Totality Magic

TRICK: Coin Disappears

Take a coin between the fingers of your right hand and announce that you will make it disappear.

Wave your left hand over the right, as if to grasp the coin with this hand [misdirection], while secretly keeping the coin in your right hand.

Shouting "Pompkins! Pompkins! In all totality!" might also help startle your audience, as you point your right index finger (still concealing the coin) to the left hand which opens up to reveal... nothing.

It also helps if you change
your name to Pompkins.

← coin remains

Persona

Traditionally, the magician adopts a stage name to inspire a certain appeal. My advice in this area: take stock of who you are, what your most interesting qualities might be, and devise a "persona" to fit.

When I became Dr Pompkins I took to wearing a stethoscope and many times was asked to perform vital surgery when out and about. I saved as many lives as those I tragically cut short… Just joking – everyone survived!

In all totality,

Dr Pompkins

CHAPTER THREE

The Costsnippas Convenience Store

Esmé made her way to the shop, thinking how she had never had this much bother over a tangerine before. She wondered why she was always the sensible one, always buying cleaning products and worrying about her watch, while the rest of her family were singing odes to pot plants, or now making string appear from crisp packets.

While Uncle Potty did the magic, Esmé's parents were self-confessed hippies – they were spiritual, enlightened, at peace with the rhythms of nature, but perhaps at odds with bringing up a very practical young daughter. They had gone on a woodland holiday as a chance to "reconnect with nature", which meant incredibly long, arduous walks for hours. As Monty and Esmé were now, at the grand old age of eleven, finding these hikes less appealing, Uncle Potty had been given the job of babysitter for the week.

Jane and Roger Pepper had first met under the light of a May Full Moon, when they had both travelled to an ancient stone circle near Penge to celebrate the Goddess of Worms (or something like that, Esmé did not quite remember). Jane had a very prominent spiritual side that manifested itself in buying Eastern religious icons, small spears of dull-coloured crystal and a great many beaded skirts. (Mr Pepper had joined in recently by growing a beard.) There were wind chimes outside the front door and a large Buddha that sat in the hallway just to the left as you came in – it was from Thailand and it had taken a considerable amount of effort to get it all the way back to London.

Monty was entirely fine with the wind chimes and the Buddha – in this respect,

Montague Pepper was his mother's son – but Esmé had always thought that the Buddha could at least have been put in a corner somewhere, which would have reduced the risk of injury to visitors.

The way Esmé saw it, the world was an incredible place already, without the need for wind chimes and rambling walks. Her parents were spiritual people, which was fine, but Esmé liked facts. That scientists could communicate with a whale was impressive, and more so because it was based on solid evidence, nothing wishy-washy. Esmé imagined having a chat with a parrot, writing a letter to a kangaroo – even sending an email to a horse. Maybe one day she would visit a beluga whale and ask just exactly what the bottom of the ocean was like. Hopefully, the whale in question would have learnt to say more than "goggles", as that could make conversation somewhat limited. Maybe by the time she got there it would have learnt to say, "I can help with your homework," or "Would you like to be a marine biologist?" in a deep, whaley voice. Esmé really hoped so.

As Esmé approached CostSnippas, the International Magic Guys (IMG) HQ opposite came into view. The building itself was impossibly old and rather dark, with battered brickwork and leaded windows. There was a crooked spire that cast a deep shadow across the road, and ugly gargoyles were situated at points along the roof edge. The huge front door was made from oak, but had warped slightly. The windows were thin and narrow. The IMG looked mysterious and out of step with the modern world. Even the hedges looked dusty.

In front of the old oak door was a statue of Barry Houdini, the IMG's founder. Houdini's most celebrated trick involved him escaping from a large wooden chest that had been dropped into the middle of the ocean. Houdini would always be shackled and chained, sometimes with a mouth full of sewing needles or maybe some razor blades. Sometimes he filled the trunk with lead, to make the trunk sink faster in the water, adding more danger. Sometimes he dangled off buildings or was "buried" under six feet of soil. He would always escape. The bronze statue outside the IMG depicted the great magician dressed in his underpants, chains round his feet, holding an open padlock aloft in victory. It was an arresting pose.

Esmé enjoyed going to the CostSnippas shop, especially if she was allowed to go on her own. Music tinkled from the radio – pop songs about driving big cars and going out on a Saturday night – but most of all, Esmé liked the new stationery shelf.

Esmé picked up an A4 lined notebook, spiral bound and sporting a green cover,

which shimmered slightly, reflecting the strip lighting above. She chose a chocolate-covered wafer bar, that had extra crunchy blue cracknel on the top, then, after a moment's thought, she bought a cleaning spray, just in case they had run out at home.

Jimi Sinha ran CostSnippas and over the years he'd often helped Esmé out with anything from difficult maths homework to practical stuff like fixing her bike. Jimi knew Uncle Potty, and Esmé thought that he might have some good advice for her on how to cope with the squashed fruit, disappearing watches and the terrible, terrible mess. Jimi watched her, wondering why she was so different from the rest of

the kids who came in here. Most of them just lingered by the sweets, although some of them came in just to steal lollies from the freezer cabinets. Esmé was happy buying paperclips and Mr Muscle.

He smiled at her as she approached the till. "Buying another?" he asked, pointing to her notebook. She had bought one only last week.

"My last notebook was ruined just now," Esmé explained. "An accident with a bowl of water and a citrus fruit."

"One of Potty's tricks gone wrong?"

"How did you guess?" Esmé replied, genuinely surprised.

Everyone in the local area knew the Potty Magician. He had spent a lifetime at the

International Magic Guys HQ, sometimes hanging out of the window performing card tricks on pigeons or trying to make the ornamental shrubbery round the building disappear.

"I don't mind a few magic tricks now and again," said Esmé, "but Uncle Potty can't stop. Plus he keeps messing things up."

Jimi looked extra pensive. He had looked through the shop window on many occasions to see Uncle Potty trying to make traffic wardens levitate. He chuckled to himself. Uncle Potty was a "wild card" – a true eccentric.

"Could he be messing up the tricks on purpose, as part of a new routine?" asked Jimi.

"I don't think so," replied Esmé. "Yesterday he tried to produce twenty tins of baked beans from a long silk scarf. There were an awful lot of beans to clean up afterwards. The living-room carpet was ruined."

Jimi scratched his left eyebrow pensively. "The tins were open?"

"Yes." Esmé warmed to her theme. "And yesterday, Uncle Potty managed to get stuck in the bathroom for an hour while he worked on his 'Underwater Sea' trick and somehow fused the boiler at the same time, so we have no hot water. Plus he's broken the door bell, my watch, damaged the Hoover trying to suck up the beans and spilt water over Mum and Dad's laptop."

"Oh, dear," mused Jimi. "My brother could look at the laptop for you and maybe the vacuum cleaner, if you bring it in. The doorbell might just need a new fuse. Not sure about the boiler – maybe Potty knows a good plumber."

Esmé shook her head. "I don't think he knows what a plumber is."

"Do you think he's nervous about the IMG performance the day after tomorrow?"

"What performance?" replied Esmé.

Jimi lowered his voice, although the only other person in the shop was a man who had been staring at light bulbs for half an hour.

"Rumour has it that the show is being put on for the Pan-Continental Magic Corporation,

who own and fund the club. If the IMG doesn't make the grade it could face the axe."

"If the IMG closes, Uncle Potty will be devastated!" said Esmé.

"I've heard the PCMC are very hard to please – in particular the boss, Nigella Spoon," said Jimi, who seemed to know a lot about the matter. "She takes a great deal of pleasure in closing down a failing club. Nigella is as hard as nails. I met her once and she trod on my toe – although she claimed it was an accident, it is hard to forget. I'm sure that she meant to do it."

Esmé was worried. If Uncle Potty's tricks were anything to go by, the whole club could be in trouble.

"If the IMG closes, each and every one of the IMG members will face financial and emotional ruin," Jimi added, looking grave. "From leader Maureen Houdini – the late Barry Houdini's daughter – to Uncle Potty, the other members, their families… so many people will be affected. It will also be a sad day for the world of stage magic, and for humanity itself. It would also hit me hard as I do the catering for all the shows from my Global Snack Tea Trolley. I need to sell my pakoras and light Thai bites."

"And when is the show?"

"Day after tomorrow," replied Jimi.

Esmé suddenly realised why Uncle Potty must be trying to invent the "trick of all

58

tricks". He must have hidden the truth about the Pan-Continental Magic Corporation from the children so as not to worry them. But the International Magic Guys was in trouble. The club meant everything to Uncle Potty, and Esmé wanted to help because she understood it was so important to him. But what exactly could she do?

Esmé was no magician herself – she could not perform a trick or do a dance to save the IMG. *But to every problem there is a solution,* she thought, and there must be a way to ensure the IMG's survival. Esmé decided to go back and talk to Monty. With his new-found knowledge of magic and her common sense they might be able to hatch a plan.

An excerpt from

Dr Pompkins – Totality Magic

TRICK: The Rising Wand

Drill a hole in one end of your wand, affix a bent paperclip and tie a rubber band round it, which you then tie round your middle finger. {See fig. 1}

If you hold your hand so as the audience will not see the rubber band, the wand inexplicably rises up.

———

Cue much applause.

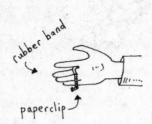

rubber band

paperclip

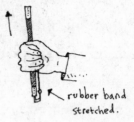

rubber band stretched.

Props

Some of you may know that in the magic world, wands have a mind of their own and rabbits appear from top hats. Danger! I cannot state it more clearly, in all matters of health and safety, that using a wand can result in very serious injury if accidentally poked in the stomach. Animals, on the other hand, are easily available and an ideal way to create magic entertainment that poses no harm at all.

In all totality,

Dr Pompkins

CHAPTER FOUR

Preparations

Esmé arrived back at Highwood Road, left her shopping bag next to the big Buddha in the hallway and ran upstairs to find Monty. He was standing in their shared bedroom with a stuffed toy elephant on his head.

"At last, my willing assistant Esmé is here," Monty announced smoothly, as if he were a well-rehearsed TV presenter who had been churned into butter and spread thickly on

toast. "Aloha, Miss Esmé Pepper. Welcome to the Hiding the Elephant trick. Come feel the weight of the elephant and let me hoist the heavy animal on to your shoulders, then see if I can make you both disappear."

It was clear that Monty's interest in magic had not abated since Uncle Potty's disastrous trick.

"Where's Uncle Potty?" asked Esmé.

"He's downstairs fiddling with the laptop. Now, I must continue – let me hoist the heavy ani—"

"Monty, I have to talk to you," said Esmé earnestly. "The IMG are in trouble. They might be closed down if we don't help them. That's why Uncle Potty's getting all his tricks wrong. He's a bag of nerves."

Monty looked crossly at his sister.

"I think that Uncle Potty would have mentioned any nerves to me," Monty replied, irritated that Esmé was interrupting his trick. "I am his new assistant, his trusted aide. I have access to the inner workings of the conjuror's mind, and would be able to tell if my own uncle was nervous or not."

"Oh, don't be so silly," said Esmé. "They have to do a big show for the Pan-Continental Magic Corporation the day after tomorrow. Jimi at CostSnippas has told me all about it."

Monty took the elephant off his head.

"And Jimi knows, because he does all the IMG catering."

Monty sighed.

"I think we should try and help," concluded Esmé.

"OK, fine," agreed Monty at last. "The International Magic Guys cannot disappear, just like that. Why don't we take out a TV advert where Uncle Potty explains the problems of the IMG, and appeals to people to donate their money to the club?" suggested Monty. "I saw something similar about sponsoring pandas."

Esmé was slightly taken aback by Monty's lack of media knowledge. "You do know it costs thousands of pounds to take out a TV advert?" she told him.

"Uncle Potty and I could write that book

about magic ourselves, so if we do that we'll get someone famous to write the introduction – like the Queen or one of Hunkatron, the boy band – then we will sell loads of copies and the money we make could pay for the ad."

"It takes a long time to write a book, get it published and earn royalties," explained Esmé, realising that her brother did not have a grasp on such realities.

Monty was thoughtful. "I could always sell my cape," he said.

Esmé meanwhile had come up with a sensible idea.

"You've got the Dr Pompkins book, right? What we should do is collect the best, most

fail-safe tricks and work on a programme that we can present to Uncle Potty. Right now he needs to focus. We can help him put together a show that can't fail to impress the PCMC."

Monty agreed enthusiastically, grabbed Dr Pompkins and set about marking its pages as Esmé crept downstairs to grab her new notebook.

Together, she and Monty started compiling the best tricks from the book, from a simple rabbit-in-hat trick to something called "The Cage of Possibilities", which involved a box inside a twirling cage and a quick change of personnel. Leafing through the book, Monty saw a trick that he wanted to perform himself – the Dairy Creamer Eye Splurge.

"Wow!" he exclaimed. "This is amazing! It's simple, but ever so good," Monty eagerly told his twin. "It requires some acting skills, which luckily I have. It's a bit gory – which people love – and it only takes one person to do it. I'm going to mark it with a special bookmark."

"Do you have a special bookmark?"

"I have a bit of fingernail, which, if I can chew it off in one piece, might do it."

Esmé sighed and tore a few strips of paper from her new notebook for Monty to use as bookmarks. She and Monty wrote down the tricks that they thought were the best, then illustrated them with a few simple diagrams.

Monty even managed to colour one of the diagrams in for further clarity, which he was quite proud of. While they were doing so there was a faint tremor from below, then a loud explosion and suddenly a hole the size of a digestive biscuit appeared in the floor less than a metre away from the Pepper twins.

"What was that?" yelled Monty.

"Uncle Potty, are you all right?" shouted Esmé, concerned.

She peered through the hole and saw Uncle Potty in the kitchen below, staring back up at her.

"What on earth…?" she asked.

"Sorry," he shouted up the hole. "Little accident with the toaster."

Esmé and Monty ran downstairs to help Uncle Potty.

"What happened?" asked Esmé.

"After looking at the laptop I became hungry," replied Uncle Potty apologetically. "I decided to make some toast and it exploded."

"It exploded?" repeated Esmé.

"Yes… the sandwich, and also the toaster. Peanut butter, wholemeal bread, bicarbonate of soda, touch of dynamite. Just went out of control."

Uncle Potty, standing amid the toast crumbs, began to wring his hands and clench his jaw. His eyebrow wiggled and his ears started to turn crimson.

"You're nervous, aren't you?" Esmé remarked.

"No, not at all!" said Uncle Potty in a high-pitched voice.

"It's the International Magic Guys, isn't it?" Esmé was direct. "Jimi at CostSnippas told me all about it. You're falling apart, Uncle Potty, your nerves are getting the better of you."

Uncle Potty stopped pretending and sat down at the table with a giant "harrumph".

"I didn't want to concern either of you with it," Uncle Potty sniffled. "But yes, the IMG is about to experience the greatest test of its talent. If we don't succeed in impressing the Pan-Continental Magic Corporation,

then we're done for! In all finality!

"It's not just me – all the IMG members are worried, including our esteemed president, Maureen Houdini," continued Uncle Potty. "That's why I wanted the trick of all tricks, but everything I do seems to result in a mess of baked beans, or spilt water… or a big explosion. Maureen has told us to keep on practising and practising until we're the best we can possibly be, but the more tricks I do the less confident I seem to become."

Uncle Potty looked glum and glanced through the kitchen window. Outside, someone was mowing their lawn. Or maybe someone else's lawn, you can never be quite sure.

"If I may suggest a plan…" said Esmé,

73

wondering whether Uncle Potty would be receptive to an outside influence. "Monty and myself have been thinking of a practical solution."

Uncle Potty raised his one furry eyebrow.

"Practical?" Uncle Potty was a stranger to that particular word.

"Yes," answered Esmé. "We have thought of some tricks, using the Dr Pompkins book, that maybe you and some of your colleagues could use. If you like them, that is."

Uncle Potty stroked his chin with a long finger.

"Hm," he said.

"Hm good? Or hm bad?" asked Esmé.

"Hm… interesting," said Uncle Potty,

thinking hard. "The performers have to meet tomorrow to work out the programme – maybe I could suggest they come here, to Highwood Road. I haven't looked at the Dr Pompkins book for a few years. I've been reading Gareth Treacle's *Magic Mayhem* lately – maybe that explains the slight... problems I've been having."

"Dr Pompkins is brilliant," said Monty. "It's got some great tricks that the other club members will really love."

Esmé turned to Uncle Potty. "Look, invite the magicians over, we'll guide them through our programme and we can all work on this together. We could even get Jimi to make some snacks for us when we get hungry. We have to save the IMG. We also have to do something before the house falls apart."

"Well, I suppose it can't hurt," said Uncle Potty.

"We can make this the best International Magic Guys show ever!" Monty trilled.

"We've got two days," said Uncle Potty, now pacing the kitchen as if caught up in some deep inspiration. "Maybe we can be as good as those smart American clubs. Yes! We must work to pull off the show of a lifetime and save the IMG!" And before Esmé or Monty could say 'abracadabra', Uncle Potty had dashed off to start making phone calls.

An excerpt from

Dr Pompkins – Totality Magic

TRICK: The Thumb Trick

Place your left thumb over the right thumb, (see fig. 1) which you have judiciously bent so only the lower half is seen.

Your left index finger hides the join. Move the left hand upwards and exclaim, "In all totality, my thumb has broken in two!"

Dress Code

There are smart dressers and scruffy dressers in any walk of life, but as a magician, you've got to make an effort. Cutting a dash will give you the edge over other performers. Plan your outfit down to the last cufflink. Velvet is all very well, but what about satin? If you've had enough of tartan, why not try a houndstooth number? Spots look good with ruffles. The thing to remember is – always to make an entrance. Be noticed, be admired.

Watch the laughter, savour the applause, enjoy the fame.

In all totality,

Dr Pompkins

CHAPTER FIVE

The "Houdini Secret"

By midday the following day, a group of magicians assembled in the living room. They included:

Deidre Lemons (animal tamer); The Great Stupeedo (human cannonball); Maureen Houdini (escapologist) and Clive Pastel (Uncle Potty's stage assistant).

Monty had been terribly upset when he was introduced to Clive, who was small and friendly. "But you have an assistant already, Uncle Potty – me!" he had wailed to his uncle.

"Union rules," whispered Uncle Potty. "He's strictly for live shows. Children aren't allowed in most of the venues we perform in."

Monty was disappointed, but there was nothing he could do.

The magicians had a cup of tea and spent hours revising the programme for the IMG show with Esmé and Monty. By three o' clock Deidre Lemons had already run through her act, which involved taking her large performing rabbit, Bernard, out of a hat. The Great Stupeedo – the human

cannonball – was now drawing the arc of his trajectory, from cannon to landing point, in Esmé's new notebook. For practical reasons he had not been able to bring his cannon into Highwood Road and so was rehearsing in theory.

"That's how I plan it, with a fifty degree curve," he explained. "Then you're sure to get the right amount of lift to begin with." Somehow Stupeedo seemed familiar to Esmé although she was sure that they had never met.

As Stupeedo and Esmé worked out angles, Clive Pastel spoke to Monty. "Let me have a look at Dr Pompkins then; it's a rare book indeed."

Monty reluctantly handed Clive the book – still smarting a little at the fact Uncle Potty had a real grown-up assistant. "I don't think I've ever seen a first edition in such good nick as this," Clive said, flicking through the pages.

"It's got some great ideas," said Monty.

"It's fantastic – I might even want to borrow it sometime," said Clive, whom Monty was warming to.

Deidre Lemons heard this and agreed that Dr Pompkins was one of the world's leading authorities on magic. "I think his tips on animal taming are still relevant. Pompkins suggests energy tablets for older animals. Is it worth getting some for Bernard, Potty?

He's six years old now, you know." Deidre had faded blonde hair and tiny feet encased in tiny red Mary Jane shoes. She was in her sixties, but still sprightly. The rabbit could easily have weighed twice as much as her.

"Oh, yes," said Uncle Potty. "Reminds me of a performing seal I knew who, once he'd reached seven years old, wouldn't go on stage unless he'd had two Mars bars, a can of cola and a packet of Lockets."

"Lockets?" asked Monty.

"For the throat. He used to get very hoarse."

Deidre started telling Esmé and Monty all about working with animals.

"In my heyday, I wore a bejewelled bikini

for my act and used to go on stage with a white tiger called Dennis. Our best trick was when Dennis would appear from a box of chocolates, complete with a hat that had been made to look like a large coffee cream. We would dance a little, then he would climb back into his cage. I also had a baby lion called Ronson who could jump through a hoop wearing a nightie and sing the theme from *Born Free*, but he suffered a lot with his feet."

Esmé was especially interested, as she had been researching the fact that animals understood certain commands and words.

"Did you ever have any trouble with your animals?" she asked Deidre.

"Big cats are difficult," she said. "It's the reason why I now have Bernard. When Dennis accidentally leapt at my throat during a tricky *pas de deux*, he had to go to the Relaxed Paws Home for Retired Performing Animals."

"How frightening!" said Monty, who was certainly intrigued.

"Yes, it was rather scary. The good thing is that rabbits won't kill you. They might bite or sulk, but they're not dangerous."

Deidre stopped and tickled the back of Bernard's neck. Maybe she wished he were a young puma or maybe a small lynx, thought Esmé. "The only problem is that Bernard's been a bit lacklustre lately," admitted Deidre.

"He keeps falling asleep."

"Props!" interrupted Uncle Potty from a corner. "I need a cage on wheels for the 'Cage of Possibilities' and a mouse costume. Quick, I'll ring the mail-order place."

"And I'll order those energy tablets for Bernard," added Deidre.

"I need some extra-strong touchpaper," added Stupeedo. "Lithuanian, I think. I'll be up like a rocket. Fifty degrees, no problem."

Uncle Potty rang the mail-order company, Trix 4 U R Us, and told them what they needed.

As he was doing so, the doorbell rang.

It was Jimi, standing by his self-created Global Snack Tea Trolley. He not only had

pakoras, but spring rolls, sushi, pizza slices and some mini pork pies. It was an impressive array and he wheeled the food into the living room.

"Maureen not here?" asked Jimi. He had put by a couple of special vegetarian pakoras for her.

"Not yet," said Clive. "She sent me a text about an hour ago saying that she was running late."

"I could call her," suggested Uncle Potty as he hung up on Trix 4 U R Us. "I need to know how to pull the cage upwards from behind the back curtain and operate the music. My trick relies on special effects."

"I need special lighting on the Basket of

Doom," said Stupeedo.

"And I usually have dry ice for the rabbit trick," rejoined Deidre.

"And only Maureen knows these things?" asked Esmé, interested.

"Yes," replied Deidre. "Barry Houdini passed on the technical information to Maureen and made her swear not to disclose the workings to anyone else. The strobe lights could be in Timbuktu for all we know. The dry ice machine could be disguised as a pot plant. She's the only one who knows how the levers and pulleys work at the IMG. It's called the Houdini secret. Maureen won't tell any of us – when it comes to loyalty she's top notch, but without her there's no actual 'magic'."

"Exactly," agreed Uncle Potty. "Without her, the show is not going to have any pizzazz."

Uncle Potty called Maureen and left a message. After an hour Stupeedo was still staring at the phone, wondering why Maureen was not ringing back. Esmé now realised where she had seen Stupeedo before – yesterday at CostSnippas, staring at light bulbs.

"It's no use, she's not replying," said Stupeedo. "Where is she?"

Just then, there was a knock at the back door.

Esmé went through to the kitchen and saw through the glass door the figure of a middle-aged woman with a heavy chain round her neck, holding an enormous padlock in one hand and a bulging plastic bag in the other. Maureen was almost exactly how Esmé had imagined, but with a plastic bag.

"Hello! Maureen here," said the IMG leader, handing Esmé the bag. By now it was almost half past four, but Maureen did not apologise for being late. "In that bag are a few badges. I haven't got long, I've an awful great deal to do."

Esmé led Maureen to the living room.

"So, we're all set?" Maureen asked the magicians. "Everyone in tiptop condition? Deidre – you know where the top hats are? Stupeedo – got your helmet sorted out?

Uncle Potty – know where the boiled eggs are?" Maureen stopped for a moment. "No, wait – Jimi – know where the boiled eggs are?"

Everyone was too surprised by the sudden appearance of the IMG president to do anything but nod. Maureen was strident, forthright and rather rushed.

"I for one have had my trunk cleaned, de-loused, oiled and sprayed," she announced. "I am, yes, I am, ready for anything. Raring to go. Happy as a sandboy. Just remember – Nigella Spoon is a mean-hearted lady and if she gets near your toes, just move out of the way. Now, I am a very busy woman and I have other matters to attend to."

Maureen started to waggle her arms in a peculiar way – Esmé would have to wait a day to see the like again– then stopped and said: "Oh, bother, this is just an ordinary house with no secret exits, isn't it? Hah ha! Where's the door the ordinary mortals use?"

Esmé pointed to the corridor and watched Maureen as she strode past the big Buddha, opened the door and let herself out.

Back in the living room, the magicians opened the plastic bag and found button badges with Maureen's smiling face printed on each one. Gleefully, they pinned the badges on. Rather than being confused by

93

Maureen's brief visit, the magicians were buoyed with excitement. Miss Houdini certainly was a charismatic woman, thought Esmé; magician royalty, almost.

Esmé took Monty aside while the IMG members busied themselves with their badges.

"We still don't know how the levers work," she told her twin. "They seem to be quite important."

"But now Maureen's made an appearance," said Monty, "everyone is that little bit more confident the show will be a success."

Esmé was insistent: "Uncle Potty says his trick is nothing without the technical stuff."

"Esmé, you worry too much. Everything

94

is ready," said Monty, with no sign of doubt. "I'd bet my cape on it."

But Esmé was not so sure.

Dr Pompkins – Totality Magic

TRICK: Find Your Card

Get yourself a pack of tapered cards (available from magic shops) and shuffle.

Ask a friend to take a card and memorise it. Then take the card (face down) and put it back in the deck, but – importantly – the other way round.

Shuffle the cards again and then ease out a card slowly. Your friend's card will naturally rise out of the deck.

Voilà!

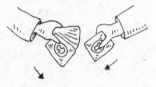

Your Audience

Despite what they might have you believe, there are only two types of audience: awake and asleep. Your job is to awaken them! I have heard one conjuror complain that his audience was "dull" or quite simply, "smelt of unwashed potatoes". Tish, now! It is your job to put the audience in a good frame of mind, not to blame them if their response is lacking. Your audience might have had a tricky time getting to the venue, or are in the middle of digesting a heavy and rather revolting supper. Give them time. Give them space. Charm them.

In all totality,

Dr Pompkins

CHAPTER SIX

The Trunk with the Secret Panel

Maureen walked up the road as if she were a buffalo storming through a wild open field. It was now early evening and the blackbirds sang an enthusiastic melody in the trees above. Maureen marched across the pedestrian crossing, not listening to the birds, all the while concentrating on the task in hand. Tomorrow, she would have to face

Nigella Spoon and the panel from the Pan-Continental Magic Corporation. Tomorrow, she had to fight to save the IMG. Tomorrow, she would need the trick of all tricks.

Miss Houdini wanted to do some preparation ahead of the show. She had a very special trunk in mind for the finale – out of all the many chests her father had passed down to her it was the strongest and the hardest to escape from or get into – from which she would perform the ultimate escape. Number twenty-seven, the "Thai trunk" was built by her father in 1949 out of solid wood from the coconut tree. The trunk was big and cumbersome, a giant beast that could easily accommodate Maureen and the two-metre length of thick "Broadmoor" chain that she had saved for special performances. The chain was impossibly weighty and – to the lay person – would provide no easy means of escape. But Barry Houdini had taught Maureen all the tricks of the trade, from the moment she had learnt to write her own name.

Performing was in Maureen's blood, although she had gone through a short teenage phase of wanting to be an astronaut. The IMG building was like a home from home – in fact it was her home; she lived above the dressing rooms in a small apartment that had been taken over somewhat by wooden trunks.

The club and headquarters had been created by Barry Houdini in 1951. A celebrated escapologist, self-publicist and champion of traditional entertainment, Houdini was once the most famous entertainer in Britain – maybe the world. But when Barry was elevated to a position of power and high status, one thing puzzled him. What to do with his oodles of cash and where to go on a Sunday afternoon? Or even a wet Wednesday?

One day he was pondering this with his good friend and fellow magician Kenny Devant, over a pint of scrumpy cider in their local pub. The pub they were sitting in was rubbish. The scrumpy was flat, the seats were hard and the landlord – who didn't like magicians and called them "deceptive types" – was always in a foul mood. And it was closed on Sunday afternoons and wet Wednesdays.

"What you need, Houdini, old pal, is somewhere we magicians could all go, any time. Somewhere inviting, comfortable – with plush furnishings and perhaps a little statuette of yourself outside. What you should build, my friend, is a Magic HQ. A club."

Houdini was delighted with the idea. "I just need a name for us all," he said, skipping over such invariably boring details as costs, paperwork, reputable builders and land registry charges.

"Why not The Globally Recognised Team Of People Who Like Performing Deceptive Tricks On The General Public Hopefully For A Reasonable Fee? The GRTOPWLPDTOTGPHFARF for short, of course," suggested Devant.

Houdini thought for a moment, twining his legs round each other as if they were curls of thick rope.

"Or maybe just – The International Magic Guys – IMG for short."

As she stepped into trunk twenty-seven Maureen glanced at the portrait of her late father on the dressing-room wall. It was painted by Picasso and executed in a way that was… almost… impressionistic. Or was it modernist? Or maybe just wrong? For Barry Houdini's face looked normal enough, but his nose had been rendered bright yellow, and in a peculiar shape, so that it resembled a Dairylea cheese triangle. Had he sported that very nose in reality? Maureen could not remember any more.

Maureen wanted to familiarise herself with the trunk before tomorrow's show. She wrapped the "Broadmoor" chain tightly round her shoulders – the huge weight of each link was strangely comforting – and clicked the padlock, which again was a soothing sound. Next Maureen lowered her body and folded it into the trunk. Barry

Houdini had last used the chest in 1975 for an impromptu show in Thailand. He was hoisted up a coconut tree and escaped in three seconds flat, appearing with a papaya in his teeth (which was quite difficult as he did not have a very wide mouth) and trousers made out of banana skins.

"The greatest trunk in the world!" he had told Maureen. She had not used this trunk for a long time, but she was confident that, like all of Barry Houdini's props, its secret mechanisms were strong. Once Maureen had secured herself inside and locked the trunk, she attempted to locate the secret panel again, but she couldn't find it. She was sure that she had lowered herself in the right way round. Maybe the panel was by her shoulders instead. She started to push the sides with her elbows, but nothing was giving way, the chest was tight against her. Maureen flicked her fingers upwards – the chains surrounding her gave way easily enough, but when she tried to open the smaller lock from the inside – which was a key feature inside every one of Houdini's trunks – Maureen simply could not locate it. Why had she thought that this was her favourite trunk? Maybe that was trunk number twenty-six... Dammit.

But Maureen did not panic. She told herself everything she'd learnt from her father: patience, deep breathing and a greater understanding of the cyclical nature of the universe – i.e. if she had got into the box, she would be able, somehow, to get out of it.

As night began to fall outside, Maureen felt sleepy. Trunk number twenty-seven was warm and cosy – and although she had wanted to test her ability to escape the trunk, the IMG leader fell asleep right inside it.

Dr Pompkins – Totality Magic

TRICK: The Bending Fork

Place in front of you a very solid, normal dinner fork. Explain to your audience how sturdy it really is.

Then hold the fork in a firm grasp with one hand, grab the handle with the other hand and tussle with the fork, claiming you can "bend" it.

If you keep your hands covering the spoon, and move the spoon back slowly, but maintain your hands as if they are holding the spoon upright, the fork looks like it's bending!

Now "unbend" the spoon by stroking it to reveal a restored piece of cutlery.

––––––

The trick is all in making the audience look at the prongs of the fork, not your hands.

front view

side view

Misdirection

The skill of magic – many people would imagine – is to have very thin arms teamed with very large sleeves. Or to look good in a bow tie. But to the true insider, the art of magic is misdirection – performing the trick while your audience's focus is elsewhere.

And with that, in all totality,

Dr Pompkins

CHAPTER SEVEN

A Strict
"No Children" Policy

Once the other magicians had left Highwood Road, Uncle Potty and Clive Pastel had continued to practise their routine. Clive made a very good spaghetti bolognese for dinner, then he and Uncle Potty rehearsed some more, improvising around the fact that they would have none of the exact props needed – or special effects

– until the show itself. The trick, as far as Esmé and Monty could make out, involved Clive as a "mouse" sitting in a box, inside a cage that was twirled round and round on its wheels by Uncle Potty and at one stage lifted high into the air – although Clive would have already secretly escaped the cage by that point and been replaced by the Great Stupeedo dressed as a lion. For the rehearsals in the living room, they had used a cardboard box on a skateboard, which did not have the right wheels, but Uncle Potty was a professional – and Clive appeared to know what he was doing.

It was getting late now, but Monty was still overly excited.

"I can't wait to see the show tomorrow!" he gasped. "The lights, the smoke, the cage... It really will be different with an audience, won't it? Maybe you could add a dragon to your show or stick Clive's hand in a giant toasted sandwich maker. I'll just go and get Dr Pompkins and see what he suggests..." replied Clive.

Clive gave Uncle Potty a stern glance.

"You have told them, haven't you?"

"Er, no," replied Uncle Potty sheepishly.

"I think now might be the time..."

Uncle Potty looked at Esmé and Monty under his eyebrow. "I'm sorry, but you won't be able to come to the IMG show tomorrow. Children are not allowed inside the building."

"What?" Esmé was flabbergasted. "After all we've done to help!"

"Sorry," replied Clive. And then, slightly annoyingly: "Them's the rules."

Esmé winced at Clive's grammar – Monty looked at Uncle Potty in disbelief. Monty had never been so disappointed. They had devised the programme with the magicians and gone through every page of the Dr Pompkins book – now they weren't allowed in to see the show.

"The problem is," explained Uncle Potty, sitting down on the sofa, his red bow tie half undone, "that the Pan-Continental Magic Corporation brought in a strict "no

children" policy a few years ago – something about safety concerns, blah blah. All those trap doors and levers…"

Esmé looked at Uncle Potty blankly. She had supposed magic was all about fun and entertainment – for grown-ups and children: everybody. You would have thought that the last place to have a no-children policy would have been a magic club.

"At least you have a Maureen Houdini badge…" said Uncle Potty, fully aware that this was not much of a consolation.

"It's not the same," said Monty crossly. "We want to come along, Uncle Potty, we deserve to…"

"It's late, I must be going," said Clive,

uncomfortable with the conversation. He was a kind man; he disliked seeing the children let down like this.

"See you tomorrow, Pots," he said, closing the front door behind him.

"Well," said Esmé, hiding her utter and absolute and enormous dismay. "If health and safety rules say we're not allowed, then we can't argue. Maybe it's better that we stay safe with all those big levers..." But even Esmé could not quite convince herself that she was happy with the arrangement.

"Please, Uncle Potty, please," said Monty. "We won't tell anyone."

Uncle Potty sat on the sofa, crossing and uncrossing his legs, trying to think his way out of the dilemma. Esmé and Monty had, in the last few days, been vital to his tricks. They had helped him prepare them, Monty had helped execute them – and they had both been good at tidying up the mess afterwards. The Pepper twins had been nothing but encouraging, even when the beans tipped on the floor and the water spilt everywhere and the boiler broke and... they had even helped devise the programme. How could he prevent the children coming to the IMG tomorrow? Only a very cruel person would deny them the greatest show on earth...

"All right, children, you can come in with me."

"Brilliant!" shouted Monty and he started

jumping up and down.

"Thanks," said Esmé, beaming.

"But only under certain conditions," said Uncle Potty. "If you are to join me you will both be in danger of being found out and you will also be at risk of possible harm from various magical contraptions, as previously discussed. Therefore, I propose:

"One. No coughing or sneezing – we don't want you being discovered.

"Two. No handling equipment – whether it looks safe or otherwise – you could be sliced in half.

"Three. No touching levers or pulleys – you might get an electric shock and be fried to cinders.

"Four. No handling animals - I once witnessed a dear friend disappear completely live on stage, never to be seen again. He was placed into a large velvet box with a tin of sardines and a very hungry polar bear and when they opened it up he was gone. Mind you, he owed the Inland Revenue a lot of money at the time…"

Esmé and Monty nodded. Instead of discouraging the children, Uncle Potty's speech had only served to make the IMG more glamorous. The very idea of danger – levers, pulleys, polar bears and sardines – was extremely exciting. Even sensible Esmé had to try hard to contain her anticipation. They were to be allowed in at last.

Dr Pompkins – Totality Magic

TRICK: More Balls

Make two plastic balls turn into three. Take two Ping-Pong balls and move them around with your fingers, from digit to digit, like the old masters do.

Another half-ball you chopped beforehand is secretly cupped over one of the balls, so when you're ready, take it out and show it, face on, to reveal an extra, mysterious sphere!

Watch those astonished faces when performing – and check there are no other magicians who knew the trick already, in your audience.

← half ball

A Solitary Life? No!

Most magicians see others as rivals. My advice? Join your local magic organisation – it provides a community for magicians and it inspires loyalty. Thus it becomes unacceptable for a performer to steal another's act when they are part of the same club. Clever stuff.

In all totality, *Dr Pompkins*

CHAPTER EIGHT

The International Magic Guys

The next day, after a long and restful night's sleep, Maureen Houdini awoke to find herself still in trunk twenty-seven. There were breathing holes at least, and room to wiggle her toes, but this was not an ideal situation to be in.

Maureen knew that Deidre, Stupeedo and Uncle Potty were scheduled to be here any minute and she dearly hoped that they could free her. Nigella's visit was fast approaching and Maureen was not going to be at her most useful stuck in a trunk. As a member of a prestigious magic club you have access to certain secrets and the condition of your membership is that you never disclose these to the public. That is accepted. But if you are the *president* of a magic club, then you are in receipt of more secrets than anyone else, especially the ones your father told you not to tell anyone else while on his deathbed after what proved to be a fatal choking incident while eating a KitKat.

Without Maureen's knowledge of the levers and technical details, today's performance was unlikely to go well. Miss Houdini dared not think that was the case, but it was true. If Maureen was not out of the trunk in an hour, the IMG was doomed.

Uncle Potty had managed to find a floor-length tweed cape, which, while looking quite odd on a warm summer's day, hid the two young Peppers very well. As they made their way to the IMG, all Esmé and Monty had to do was scurry in time with Uncle Potty's feet, without tripping over. Esmé envisioned scuffed knees at any moment now and so was pleased that she had remembered to bring some plasters with her.

The first few minutes of the journey had

been tricky, but soon the Peppers found the right pace. Esmé had never travelled this way before. She had suspected the world of subterfuge and deception to be fraught with guilt and bad feeling, but in fact she was enjoying it.

When they got to the IMG HQ, there was a long queue of people already waiting to get in. The show was open to anyone who could get a ticket, and a handful of interested magicians who wanted to see the International Magic Guys in full effect. A few people recognised Uncle Potty – they had seen his shows before – and he waved to them enthusiastically.

"Hello!" he said. "It's going to be one

jelly-belly humdinger this afternoon!" No one noticed that Uncle Potty had two extra sets of legs or, if they did, they assumed this might be part of his act.

A high, tinkling bell rang and the audience began to shuffle into the venue. Uncle Potty walked towards the "performer's entrance" and Esmé and Monty slipped into the building with no trouble at all.

"To the backstage area!" cried Uncle Potty as the Peppers emerged from his cape. "Via the props department."

Esmé and Monty saw that they had arrived in a vast room that held various IMG contraptions. But these were not small, spindly little tables or tiny cabinets you could fit inside a wooden box. Before them was an array of towering objects, some bigger than the biggest Egyptian stone in the British Museum.

"It's all... simply... gigantic!" gasped Monty. This was another side of magic completely – a world away from close-up, magic performed to a small gathering of people. This was the world of the big stadium show. In the half-light Esmé and Monty could see a tall guillotine, set up for a trick. Uncle Potty told them it was, rather chillingly, known as "The Murderer".

Esmé shivered. Even Monty looked fearful.

"It's extremely Victorian," said Uncle Potty, matter-of-factly. "Firstly you slice an apple in half to show that the guillotine is fully working. Then, after some well-rehearsed patter with your assistant, he or she admits to the theft of a huge diamond, blah blah. The assistant looks a bit remorseful, but then you invite an audience member to come on stage and look for the diamond. Of course, they find it not on the assistant, but on their own person! You subject the audience member to the guillotine and they lean their head on the wooden neck rest. With a bit of drama the blade comes down and it looks as if the innocent person's head falls off."

"Wow!" Monty gasped.

130

Esmé was equally amazed.

Potty spoke plainly. "What happens is that while the audience member puts their head on the guillotine, no one notices the assistant quickly remove the blade – although your participant is obviously made aware of this in case of heart attack, etc."

"But what about the head?" asked Esmé. "You said that it falls off."

"The magician holds a fake papier-mâché head in his jacket and as the 'blade' comes down he lets it drop to the floor and quickly covers the shoulders with a cloth," replied Potty. "You just have to remember to choose an audience member who has the same colour hair as the one on the papier-mâché model."

"That's amazing," said Monty, walking up to the guillotine, just to see what it might feel like to put his head on it.

"Careful now!" shouted Uncle Potty. "You are well served to remember the list of rules I gave you last night."

Monty backed away and Uncle Potty moved them to another part of the room where stood an enormous goldfish bowl, which in itself was magnificent, without the children even knowing what it might be used for on stage.

"In the old days a magician would fill the glass bowl up with water," explained Uncle Potty. "Then he or she would reveal a giant goldfish, swimming around – which was an

illusion in itself. Then the magician would get into the bowl and suddenly it would be dry inside and the goldfish turned into a dragon. In a variation the magician might "slay" the dragon, then add noodles and pass round this delicious "dragon soup" to members of the audience. Sometimes the assistant might add a real shark to the water for extra danger. The bowl's uses are manifold."

Uncle Potty moved to the rear wall, where there stood a collection of tall mirrors hinged together.

"Then there's the hall of mirrors, in which you can hide most of your audience, an elephant or maybe even a lorry full of cobras. You can make anything disappear – at different angles the mirrors reflect and also hide different parts of the stage. Mirrors are still the first port of call for the modern illusionist, although the idea goes back centuries."

"That's right," said Monty, the idea dawning on him like a spectacular sunrise. "I saw a video on the internet of a cat who seemed to disappear in mid-air – that must have been through mirrors."

"Yes, it most probably was," said Uncle Potty. "Highly persuasive."

"That's magic, isn't it?" Esmé responded, who was beginning to see just how exact these performances had to be. "Persuading people to suspend their disbelief. So… you have to get all the angles right with the mirrors – and the timings right with the guillotine. And the projections of goldfish have to be realistic and bang on time."

Esmé pondered for a moment more. "Now I see why you need Maureen's technical know-how. It's not just patter, it's all the behind-the-scenes action and split-second timing."

"Exactly!" said Uncle Potty. "It's how you create the mystery! Everyone wants to believe in magic. There are very few people who would wish the magician to fail. Your audience want to feel that expectation, revel in the tension, their own anxiety and nervousness. Sometimes they want blood and gore! Sometimes they need plain silliness and hats made out of sausages. A magician's job is to deceive, yes, because the audience *wants* to be deceived."

By now, Uncle Potty was fiddling with a light switch on the side of the wall.

"If you turn the lights on, someone might discover us," Esmé warned.

"No, no, this is not a normal light switch," said Uncle Potty. "I am trying to find the way to…"

"Where?" asked Monty.

"To the dressing rooms… It's just… the concealed exit…" Uncle Potty wiggled the switch and then thumped the wall.

Monty put his hand out and instinctively located what looked like a shelf and lightly tapped it. A small panel in the wall slid open just like in an action movie.

"Come along, Esmé and Monty, no time to waste," said Uncle Potty as he made his way through the exit. "And remember, if anyone sees you your heads will end up on that very guillotine!"

Esmé and Monty gulped and slipped inside the cape with Uncle Potty, and into the next room. The twins would have to stay undetected for the whole day and that was not going to be easy. Esmé dreaded to think what would happen if they were found out.

An excerpt from

Dr Pompkins – Totality Magic

TRICK: Buried Treasure Box

Find a small box with a concealed compartment in a local magic shop.

One moment, the box will be empty; flick a switch and now it is filled with organic peanuts! Or treasure! Or whatever you fancy.

If your catchphrase is "Who buried all the treasure?", and your persona is a bit pirate-y, you'll cause a sensation.

Remember, you can tailor your act at all times to make it your own.

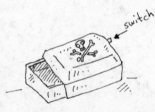

switch

Your Catchphrase

There is nothing wrong in having a catchphrase as long as it is original and not too long. I invented "in all totality" on a long walk to a particularly exquisite patisserie down Basingstoke way. Similarly, Pat Daniels's "You're going to like it, not a lot, but you'll like it," was invented when he was grouting his bathroom.

In all totality,

Dr Pompkins

CHAPTER NINE

Stuck

On the other side of the magic door, Uncle Potty and the Peppers found themselves by the dressing rooms. "Let's see how the boss is doing," muttered Uncle Potty, adjusting his Maureen badge and knocking politely on her dressing room.

There was no reply, so Uncle Potty opened the door, which gave a huge creak, and entered.

140

"Maureen?"

Uncle Potty spotted the locked trunk on the floor. "Maureen?" he enquired of the trunk. "Are you in there?"

The trunk knocked twice. Maureen had realised that speaking was of no use and knocking was the clearest form of communication.

"Is she all right?" Esmé whispered up to Uncle Potty through the woollen folds of the cape, which were – inexplicably – beginning to emit the smell of smoked mackerel.

"Are you all right?" Uncle Potty asked the trunk, which again knocked twice.

"It shows she still has oxygen," said Esmé.

Uncle Potty lowered his chin and

141

whispered at his cape: "Come out, children. Maureen can't see you."

Esmé and Monty appeared. It was somewhat of a relief: the mackerel smell was getting a bit much.

"Is it once for yes and twice for no?"

"I think it's the other way round," whispered Esmé. "I saw it in a survival show. More complicated to knock for yes. Proves you've not lost your mind in times of stress and reduced oxygen."

The three visitors stared at the trunk for some time, as if waiting for it to do something, although it quite clearly was not going to do anything at all.

"Do you think she's rehearsing, or do you

think she's stuck?" asked Esmé quietly.

"I don't know," said Uncle Potty, his brow furrowing like a well-ploughed field.

"Why don't you ask?" Esmé nudged Uncle Potty.

"Are you, ahem, stuck, Maureen?"

The trunk knocked twice.

Immediately, Uncle Potty started to fret. "The IMG president cannot be stuck in a trunk. We need her skills for the show."

There was a knock at the dressing-room door; Esmé and Monty rushed under Uncle Potty's cape, as Deidre and Stupeedo entered the dressing room together.

"Good news! Trix 4 U R Us have just delivered our order – your cage and the mouse costume are here. Stupeedo's touchpaper and Bernard's energy tablets have arrived safely too," said Deidre brightly. Then she noticed the look on Uncle Potty's face. "What's going on?"

"Maureen's locked herself in the trunk," said Uncle Potty.

"Oh," said Deidre. "Oh, dear," and she rushed towards the ancient wooden chest and started to examine it. "Trunk number twenty-seven, the Thai trunk. It's notoriously temperamental. Maureen, are you OK?"

Stupeedo quickly became agitated. Normally he suffered with nerves before a show, but he was finding it hard to contain himself.

"Deidre, I need the extra-long matchsticks

and I've no idea where they are, whether they're in a drawer or a cupboard or a secure lock-up off the Marylebone Road," he babbled. "I need to polish my helmet with a really soft cloth... I need at least two cups of tea and half a packet of Jammie Dodgers plus some reassurance and maybe some nice-smelling candles. Those purple ones. And some rescue remedy mouthwash."

Stupeedo ran up to the trunk. "Maureen, can't you possibly come out? Wiggle your toes and open the lock from inside?"

The trunk knocked once.

"She really *is* stuck," said Deidre, who had now carefully examined each side of the trunk.

Stupeedo started panicking, and small bits of spittle formed at the sides of his mouth.

"I don't believe it! The most important day in the IMG's calendar and we're ruined!"

Deidre remained by the side of the trunk. "You must stay calm, Nigel. We've just got to think of a plan."

From her vantage point near the floor, Deidre had noticed Uncle Potty's cape.

It was moving.

Deidre didn't say anything at first, thinking that this might be a trick of the light. But what if Uncle Potty had Maureen hidden under that unusually long cape, and was pretending she was locked in the trunk as a practical joke? Deidre did not like practical jokes.

"What's in your cape, Potty?" she asked.

"Er, nothing," came Uncle Potty's weak reply.

In a flash, as if she had been plugged into the mains, Deidre leapt at Uncle Potty's cape and pulled it open to reveal...

"Esmé and Monty!"

The children stepped out into the light of the dressing room, which was not that light at all.

"You're not allowed in here," Deidre was exasperated. "It's against the rules. Nigella will definitely fail us if she sees you anywhere within the IMG."

"I thought that the children might be of some help," said Uncle Potty. "They were so good yesterday, and so keen to see the show…"

Deidre gave Uncle Potty a stern look. "What were you thinking of? Maureen's stuck in a trunk and now you bring two illegal children into the IMG."

Deidre addressed the trunk – she was not going to give up yet.

"Maureen, we are going to do everything we can to make sure you're out of the trunk before Nigella arrives. We also know that you know that there are two children in the IMG. Do not worry, I will get rid of them."

Esmé and Monty looked horrified.

"Next, we will have to hack into the trunk with a hatchet—"

"Deidre," interrupted Esmé softly.

Miss Lemons ignored her and carried on talking to the trunk.

"If that doesn't work we could use a small explosive…"

"Deidre," said Esmé again. "I have an idea."

Deidre turned to Esmé. "The rules do not permit children in the building. I can't make any exceptions, not today."

"But listen to this: maybe the trunk has a spare key."

Deidre hadn't thought of this – neither

149

had Uncle Potty, Stupeedo or Monty.

"Maybe you're right, Esmé," mused Deidre. "There is a box full of keys in the Secret Escapology room. Barry Houdini was always known for covering himself in all eventualities – it's a good suggestion. The key to this trunk would be clearly marked 'Houdini Number twenty-seven'."

"Great," said Esmé, hoping that this might keep herself and Monty in the IMG for a little longer.

"It's such a shame you can't stay for the afternoon…" said Deidre sadly. "But we will be in so much trouble…"

Uncle Potty had to concede and told Deidre: "I'll show the kids out through the

back exit then head up to the Escapology room and look for the key."

"Be as quick as you can," said Deidre. "The audience will be seated by now."

"Rightio," replied Uncle Potty. "Your word is my commode."

Esmé was disappointed, but there was nothing she could do. She and Monty were not wanted in the IMG, they were too much trouble.

Uncle Potty led the children through another dusty corridor to the back exit, which was filled with gadgets and magic props from the last 150 years, some in glass containers, others in display cabinets. Rather than rushing out, Monty kept stopping to look at each item one by one.

"Look, it's Ellie Baba's famous biroscope! Look through it and it produces a drawing of you 'innermost thoughts' in ballpoint pen!"

"Come along, Monty," called Uncle Potty.

"And here's Kevin Kebabra's revolving bow tie! Apparently, if you stare at it for long enough with half-closed eyes, it shows the word 'bonkers'."

"Monty, I said hurry up."

"Look, Esmé, a stuffed baboon! The one that played the piano in Las Vegas with its toes—"

"Montague Pepper, please refer to the rules I gave you... but, um, unfortunately did not write down!" shouted Uncle Potty.

152

Monty felt the power of those rather wonderful museum pieces. He felt the seriousness of entertainment, the gravity of the glorious wonder of magic. He also felt a bit dizzy, and wondered if this had anything to do with having been sat inside Uncle Potty's cape, which still smelt of smoked mackerel.

As Monty caught up with Esmé and Uncle Potty there was a noise – someone's voice? – coming from the back exit.

Uncle Potty stopped at once and Monty nearly ran into him.

"Oh, no!" gasped Uncle Potty. "Nigella Spoon!"

"What are we going to do?" said Esmé in

a low voice. "If she sees us…"

"…she'll go crazy, yes," Uncle Potty finished.

Esmé gasped and got back inside the cape. Monty looked panicked as he did the same. He wondered if Nigella would really use the guillotine on him.

Uncle Potty walked towards the door, hesitant.

"Ah, Nigell— oh, Clive, what are you doing? Why are you so late?"

"Sorry, overslept," said Clive, hurrying into the backstage area, looking tired and frazzled. "I spent most of the night going over the cage trick. I twirled myself about in a cardboard box for hours and I still feel a bit light-headed. Everything OK?"

Should Uncle Potty mention the fact that Maureen was stuck in a trunk backstage and that there were two uninvited children inside his voluminous cape?

"Fine!" lied Uncle Potty, who didn't want to worry his small assistant. "Why don't you make yourself comfortable in one of the dressing rooms while I go up and, um, find a something, eh?"

Before Clive could ask Uncle Potty if he was being deliberately vague, a shrill voice sounded out in the corridor.

"Bernard! Come back here!"

Uncle Potty turned round to see a rabbit, who had just been fed a few too many energy

tablets in Deidre's dressing room, speeding up the hallway and disappearing. Deidre ran along a few seconds behind.

"Have you seen Bernard?" she asked Uncle Potty. "He's out of control. Those damned tablets!"

"No, I haven't," came a broad American accent from behind them. "Is he a conjuror or an illusionist? We can't have any undisciplined magicians in the show."

Everyone – apart from Bernard, who was nibbling at leftover biscuit crumbs behind a standard lamp in the corner somewhere – stopped in their tracks. Nigella was wearing an expensive skirt suit in cream linen, black patent shoes – which were rather pointy, of course – and wore her brunette hair in a sharp bob. She removed her oversized sunglasses, put them in her handbag and peered at the magicians.

"Er, Nigella! So nice to see you," said Deidre, smiling falsely at the leader of the Pan-Continental Magic Corporation. "Did you travel well? I'm Deidre Lemons, animal tamer."

"We decided to come in the back way," Nigella grimaced, equally falsely. She spoke with a cut-glass New Hampshire accent. "It wouldn't do for us to mix with the general public." Both women shook each other's hand. Deidre gingerly moved her feet away from Nigella's pointy shoes.

"These are my colleagues: Mr Yentovitz, Mr Miracle and the Incredible Gladstone – who have come all the way from New York, Hong Kong and Tasmania respectively," said Nigella. The men nodded in unison. Yentovitz was carrying an electronic tablet device, which was another thing that unnerved Deidre. He paused to make a note of something and looked up again.

"Is this person, Bernard, OK?" asked Yentovitz.

"Oh, yes, not a problem," replied Deidre.

Nigella spotted Clive and started to give him a list of her coffee requirements. Uncle Potty thought that now was a good time to nip to the secret escapology room. Perhaps, he reasoned, he could leave the children in there for a few hours until it was safe for them to leave.

Deidre grabbed Potty by a tweedy shoulder and whispered loudly in his ear.

"Have you found the key?"

"I'm on my way there now."

"Have the children gone?"

"Yes," Uncle Potty lied. For the second time.

"Thank goodness!" Deidre smiled. "That was one extra thing I couldn't deal with."

Uncle Potty motioned to walk away, Esmé and Monty hardly daring to breathe under all that tweed. Deidre grabbed him again.

"What am I going to do about Bernard, Potty?"

"Excuse me," Nigella interrupted. "Could you show me to my seat, please. And if you could let Maureen Houdini know I'm here, I'd like to see her before the show."

"Of course, madam," said Deidre, overly polite. "Not a problem. Maureen Houdini, yes. Give me a moment…"

An excerpt from

Dr Pompkins – Totality Magic

TRICK: The Magnetic Pencil

Place a pencil on a flat surface in front of you.

Now clasp your right wrist with your left hand, keeping your left index finger under the palm where it can't be seen.

Let your right hand hover over the pencil and magically it lifts up!

When you let go, the pencil drops.

What you are doing is holding the pencil with the hidden index finger, but your chums can examine the item afterwards and if they do not spot any glue, they will think you're the cat's pyjamas!

Keeping Your Cool

They say that a cat has nine lives – well, a magician has many more. A trick might go wrong, props might fall over, lines may be forgotten, but every entertainer knows that the show must go on.

It takes great experience to lock yourself in things or to swim with sharks. Unless you have been practising for twenty years or more, keep your tricks simple and safe. However, my point is that even if you are doing a trick with an old toothpick – if it goes wrong, carry on. Take it easy, smile, and move on to the next trick. Or just pretend to faint and some kindly person will drag you away.

In all totality,

Dr Pompkins

CHAPTER TEN

Secret Escapology

Deidre led Nigella and the panel to their specially selected seats in the auditorium, which was now full. Although they had never previously met, Nigella was already giving Deidre the creeps. The PCMC leader had the air of a headmistress who has just been given an extra-large detention book and a new biro at the start of the Autumn term. There was an element of smugness in her

164

shoulders, a faint smile of indifference on her lips and the cool stare of a motorcycling fox. Deidre also worried that Nigella was going to step on her toes.

Mr Yentovitz, Mr Miracle and the Incredible Gladstone were polite enough, but seemed confused by the International Magic Guys. Deidre had heard that some of the other Pan-Continental Magic Corporation clubs were all rather slick and had posh carpets. The Dubai Dibblers club was situated on the 293th floor of a skyscraper, for instance, and was said to have panoramic views of most of the Eastern hemisphere. In contrast, the IMG was eccentric and smelt a bit musty, but she hoped that the state of the building would not affect Nigella's judgement today. She wanted Nigella to be "blown away" by the performance this afternoon, rather than the soft furnishings. However, Deidre was finding it hard to remain optimistic.

"Deidre Lemons, my chair smells of mildew," said Nigella after she had sat down.

"In my opinion the carpets are also quite scruffy and the walls need painting. This could affect both the members' morale and health and safety regulations."

"I'm sure Maureen will answer your queries," replied Deidre, who knew only too well that Maureen was otherwise engaged.

"You see, it could be a sign of a club gone sour." Nigella said those last four words with

an exhaustion born from overuse. Magic clubs, in Nigella's world, were always going sour. It was the same with restaurants going sour, gym classes going sour, dreams going sour – plus parklands, train operators and newsagents, which could all go sour at any point. The only thing that never went sour in Nigella's opinion was Nigella's own opinion.

"OK, I see." A small piece of glass entered Deidre's heart. Had Nigella already given up on the IMG before the show had even begun? Had she crossed the club off the list before even stepping through the door? Everybody knew that the IMG was not modern, but surely it had its charms? Of course, HRH Prince Keith had famously become a member when he was twenty-one, having swotted up on a paltry card trick that wasn't really up to much. But his mother was the Queen, and Maureen Houdini had thought that she might be beheaded – or imprisoned in a tower or something – if she didn't let him in, so he was duly given a certificate and badge and they never saw him again.

"Got him!" Clive was in the hallway and had just caught Bernard.

Deidre was stressed and needed to breathe, but Deidre didn't have time to breathe, so she sucked a big section of air into her lungs and held it in. Deidre had sucked in air once before at a swimming competition in 1987, and had won, so she felt confident that it would work this time too.

"My chair is now creaking," Nigella told Deidre.

"I can assure you, Miss Spoon, it's our finest available chair." Deidre was not lying. All the other chairs were worse.

There was a big splintery noise that sounded a bit like a tree tripping over a loose paving stone and then deciding to sue the council.

"Arghhh!" came the accompanying human noise.

All eyes turned on The Incredible Gladstone, who had fallen through his chair.

"You see, Miss Spoon, our finest available chair."

Nigella looked despairingly at Deidre, who moved to pick up Gladstone. Deidre tried to reach his arm, but it was too far away, so she did something that most people would call "ill-advised" and "badly-timed" and "rather silly". Deidre tried to pull The Incredible Gladstone up by his leg.

No one would have been able to do it, not even a special leg-pulling robot or a truck or an elephant on steroids. Gladstone simply moved along the floor two centimetres closer and howled with pain.

"Argh!" came Gladstone's cry. "Even my time in the wilderness in Tasmania with the Tazzy Devils nipping at my elbows and the mosquitoes nibbling my knees and two hundred people to entertain with no magic wand and half a deck of cards while I wore a pair of shorts that were too tight was better than my time on this chair!"

"Get the man upright, will you?" barked Nigella, and Yentovitz immediately snapped into action, gripping Gladstone under the shoulders and heaving him up in a swift shovelling motion. Gladstone – not a young man – stood still and looked bewildered. What could he sit on without fear of personal injury?

Deidre took a few minutes to find him a solid-looking wooden stool from the office. They were all running late and she needed to get changed for the show.

"You'll have to excuse me," said Deidre, trying to feel relaxed, positive and in complete control. "I am confident and looking forward to you looking forward to the show, which we personally are all looking forward to."

Deidre wished she hadn't just said that.

"Why, thanks," said Nigella coolly, as Yentovitz wrote something down in his electronic note-taker.

Meanwhile, Uncle Potty, Monty and Esmé ascended the stairs under the aromatic cape. Once they reached the first floor and were away from view, the children popped out again.

"Look, a golden door!" gasped Monty. "The secret escapology room?"

"No, that's the cleaning cupboard," said Uncle Potty. "Follow me."

The Peppers followed as Uncle Potty took a sharp left turn, then another, then a short walk down a thin corridor and another sharp left. They seemed to be back where they started.

"The golden door…?" asked Esmé.

"Yes, this is it! The secret escapology room. Let's go right in."

Esmé decided not to mention the fact that a minute ago it was the cleaning cupboard.

Inside, the room was large and piled high with hundreds of old-fashioned suitcases,

some tightly closed, some with their contents spilling out of them as if they yearned to break free. Some cases were marked – one said "chains: light", another "chains: medium heavy", another "probably". One was marked "padlocks", one "string", one "sewing needles: blunt". There were cases of different sizes and many colours. One brown suitcase contained a pile of books, with titles such as *Fifty Best Chains* and *Ropes I Have Known* in it. Was there anything marked "keys"?

"I'll take the left side of the room, Monty the right and Esmé the middle," instructed Uncle Potty. "Go through the cases quickly. We don't have much time."

Esmé and Monty started scrambling for the suitcases. Some of the cases were piled precariously high and the children hoped that they would not topple over. After some searching, Uncle Potty soon spotted a large red attaché case that was – yes – filled with keys.

"Aha!" he cried.

"Well done," said Esmé. "Now, let's search for the right one."

With a flick of the lock the contents were revealed. Esmé and Monty gasped at the sheer amount of keys there were. They all leant over the case in wonder. The keys glistened like jewels, glinting and winking. The case was completely full and Esmé was confident that there would be something in the whole collection that would help rescue Maureen.

"So many shapes, so many colours," said Monty in awe.

"Are any of them labelled?" asked Esmé.

"Found it!" said Monty, excitedly picking up a large, ornate key and twirling it in his fingers.

"My goodness, well done!" said Uncle Potty. "Have you read the inscription?"

"Not yet, it's very small writing," answered Monty.

"Let me look," said Uncle Potty, taking the key from Monty. "Ah yes, it quite clearly, um, says... It is small writing, eh? Um..."

Uncle Potty squinted, trying to make out the lettering. "Surely it says Houdini number twenty-seven and our search is over. Maybe? Probably."

"In all totality we've found it!" cheered Monty.

Esmé thought that she should double check, took the key from Uncle Potty's hand and turned it over twice.

"It says 'Designers at Debenhams'," she announced sadly. "Why did you think it was this one, Monty?"

"I felt the Pompkins mega waves," said Monty matter-of-factly. Esmé wrinkled her nose.

"Alas!" said Uncle Potty. "But chin up,

Peppers, let's look some more," and again thirty fingers started scrabbling at the keys.

After ten minutes they had drawn a blank. Nothing read "Houdini Number twenty-seven" – all the keys were either too big, or like house keys, or marked "safe" or "admin" or were made of coloured plastic.

"None of these keys will fit the trunk lock," said Esmé.

"How do we know?" asked Monty. "We should try them all."

Bring bring! – a telephone. Uncle Potty walked over to a blue suitcase sitting in the corner on top of a pile of old magazines, opened it and answered the telephone that was inside.

"Yes, of course. Down in a minute."

Uncle Potty replaced the receiver and turned to the children. "I have to go now – Deidre says they're having a last-minute planning meeting."

Monty and Esmé were still surprised that there was a phone inside a suitcase.

"Maureen thought it would be handy to put a telephone in here in case anyone needs assistance," explained Uncle Potty.

"Maybe she should have put one inside trunk twenty-seven," said Esmé.

Uncle Potty moved to the back of the room.

"We'll stay here and look for the key a little longer," said Monty.

"But no!" cried Uncle Potty. "You could be stuck in here for a whole day! I may not be able to come back until early evening."

"Are you sure?" Esmé asked her brother. "Maybe we should go with Uncle Potty."

"If we get hungry or thirsty," noted Monty. "We could eat some chains, like the great El Gutso."

"Who was El Gutso?" asked Esmé.

"The famous Yorkshire clown," replied Monty, with some authority. "He's mentioned in Dr Pompkins. He used to eat bicycles, spanners and once a very long bridge that went over the M1, although it took him around a month."

"What's he doing now?" Esmé enquired.

"I think he works in Boots," replied Monty.

Uncle Potty started waggling his arms again.

"What are you doing?" asked Monty.

"I'm trying to activate the lasers that make the trapdoor work," explained Uncle Potty. "This connects to a chute that lands me backstage."

Esmé remembered Maureen had similarly "waggled" before she left for the "door the ordinary mortals use" at Highwood Road.

"Go on, Uncle Potty, let us come with you," implored Esmé. "We make a good a team."

Uncle Potty stopped waggling and thought for a moment. The Peppers certainly had a

182

lot of good ideas. He didn't like to see the children miss the show…

"The chute is a way we can get backstage without being seen by Nigella," added Esmé. "It makes sense."

"Aha," said Uncle Potty.

"Aha?" said Monty, quickly realising that it was better to go with Uncle Potty than stay and look for the key.

"OK, let's do it," said Uncle Potty. "You've proved quite good at hiding. Monty and Esmé, join me and let's waggle our arms together!"

Esmé and Monty joined Uncle Potty and waggled furiously. Within seconds the floor fell away beneath their feet and the trio

183

found themselves zooming down a long, winding tube in absolute darkness.

An excerpt from

Dr Pompkins – Totality Magic

TRICK: The Moving Egg

Tell your friends you can blow a whole egg from one wine glass to another using just a straw. Sounds impossible?

Well, not if you make two small holes either end of the egg and empty the contents first.

Then blow the egg easily and astoundingly. No one will ever know!

———

Not unless you tell them.

Of Your Own Invention

So where do all these new tricks come from? I urge you, dearest amateur magician, to find new ways of presenting old tricks. Make yourself a different sort of wand from the traditional type, with tassels on, or buttons. Maybe you would like to make a live badger appear from a paper cup, not just a stream of confetti? Maybe blow a pebble from one glass to another? Customise the tricks you have already learnt! Use your imagination, friends.

In all totality,

Dr Pompkins

CHAPTER ELEVEN

The Greatest Show on Earth

"Whooahhhh!" Three people arrived in a heap on Deidre Lemons's dressing-room floor.

"Sorry," said Uncle Potty. "Wasn't quite sure where we'd end up."

Deidre had changed into a sequinned dress, high heels and was wearing a tiara.

"You told me that the children were gone."

Deidre was confused and disappointed.

"Um…" Uncle Potty could not think of a good excuse, other than he'd accidentally glued the Pepper twins to his arms and could not get rid of them.

"Uncle Potty, have you got the key?" asked Clive, popping his head round the door. "Deidre told me all about it."

"Its whereabouts remain a mystery," Uncle Potty admitted.

"This is a real disaster," sighed Deidre. "No Maureen, no key, no special effects and two illegal children… While you were gone Stupeedo, Clive and I did some talking. If we are to make this show go with a bang, everyone needs to help out."

188

Deidre looked at Esmé and Monty. "Maybe the fact that you two are still here is a blessing in disguise," she said. "It's all hands on deck."

"What's the plan?" asked Uncle Potty.

"Right," Deidre said. "I need you to play music during my act, to add atmosphere. Clive is going to operate the lights from the side of the stage."

"Where's Stupeedo?" asked Uncle Potty.

"He's decided to do a bit of 'warm-up' before the show begins. He's on stage telling a joke about a shrimp and a turtle."

Uncle Potty had heard Stupeedo's jokes before and truly hoped that this one was better. Usually they had the effect of driving people away, not "warming them up".

Deidre turned to Esmé and Monty.

"I propose that as you're both still here, you can continue to try and get Maureen out of the trunk, just in case she can escape for the grand finale."

"But how?" asked Esmé.

"I haven't worked that bit out yet." said Deidre.

"What do criminals use on TV programmes to pick locks?" asked Monty.

"Hairgrips!" replied Esmé, excited. "This is the answer!"

All eyes turned to Deidre and her coiffured head, which contained more hairgrips than a West End musical.

"OK, you can have some of mine..." she said, taking three from her static hair. "Do your best – try and get Maureen out."

"Now we've got a show to do," Uncle Potty said. "No time to lose."

Deidre picked up Bernard's hutch and she, Uncle Potty and Clive walked out of the dressing room ready for the show to begin leaving Esmé and Monty behind to deal with the trunk.

Nigella Spoon had been waiting over fifteen minutes for the International Magic Guys show to start and she was becoming impatient. Nigella was not usually made to hang about this long.

Just as the PCMC leader started yawning, a bald man clad in lycra, wearing an extremely shiny helmet, took to the stage. He then proceeded to tell a joke about a shrimp and a turtle. The joke was not funny, but some of the audience liked it and Nigella felt that perhaps – although this was a tiny perhaps – this was a sign that the club at least was trying to provide a broad sweep of entertainment.

The curtains opened two minutes after Stupeedo's punchline, revealing a smiling Deidre Lemons standing next to a small felt table with a huge top hat placed on it. The lights did not dim as everyone expected, but a strong spotlight suddenly hit the table and a tin whistle started playing a basic melody in

the background.

"Welcome to the greatest show on earth!" announced Deidre, who was a little bit nervous now she was in front of an audience.

"I have before me a very ordinary top hat," Deidre's voice wavered and the sequins on her dress quivered along.

The hat had been placed over a hole in the table; the top of the hat had a hole in it too, so Deidre could see directly into the secret compartment under the table that housed Bernard. The rabbit was looking a bit dozy. Deidre wondered if the energy tablets had completely worn off by now and that was why he seemed to be going to sleep. She hoped not.

"A very ordinary top hat, but one that is very useful and good for wearing to high-falutin' events." Deidre picked up the hat, without revealing the hole in the top, and waved it around as if she frantically loved top hats and always wore one to high-falutin' events.

"When I was a child," she said, her patter thoroughly rehearsed, "I used to dream of having a pet. A fluffy friend I could call my very own."

Deidre looked out, smiled at the audience for three seconds as she always did, then looked back at the hat. Uncle Potty carried on playing the tin whistle as if there was no tomorrow. However, its high tones and

rasping dreariness were starting to grate on everyone's nerves. Soon Deidre was the only one in the room who wanted him to continue – if he suddenly stopped playing she worried that someone might hear Bernard snore.

"Did I want a dog? Did I want a cat? No! I wanted a lovely bunny rabbit!" she continued, smiling broadly, going through the motions.

Deidre secretly wondered whether this fail-safe, traditional trick had actually become rather old-fashioned. How many people in the audience would care that as a girl she had once wanted a cutesy-wootesy bunny rabbit? Would it be better if she had once wanted an enormous panther?

Deidre plunged her hand deep inside the top hat in an attempt to get Bernard out. The rabbit, however entirely asleep, was not budging. Deidre tugged, but he would not move.

"*Et voilà*," said Deidre, thinking French might help. "A lovely, fluffy bunny."

Deidre pulled more, but Bernard was not having any of it. He had grown so big he was impossible to move.

"Come on, little bunny wunny!" yelled Deidre and she tugged at Bernard's full girth.

"Easy does it!" she added as the audience started to wonder what was going on.

Deidre knew there was nothing for it but

197

to yank Bernard out as hard as she could. She whispered, "Sorry to have to do this!" then grabbed Bernard and pulled him out with all her strength. As Bernard's feet cleared the rim of the hat, he bit her on the hand.

"Ouch! Bernard!"

Bernard jumped down and scampered off the stage and on to the laps of the front row. Uncle Potty saw all this happening and started to play the tin whistle louder, faster and really quite badly. Stupeedo, who was standing by him in the wings, put his fingers in his ears.

"My goodness! A rabbit!" said a surprised audience member, as Bernard hopped from lap to lap.

Nigella thought the name Bernard sounded familiar. Wasn't he the magician who had gone missing previously? She leant over to Yentovitz. "Coincidence, two entities called Bernard?" she muttered. Yentovitz made an electronic note.

Deidre leapt off the stage, broke a heel, hobbled over to Bernard and pulled him from the front row. She ran back up to the stage lopsidedly, curtsied, while trying not to sob uncontrollably, and exited stage left.

"That was an epic failure!" she wailed to Stupeedo, putting Bernard back in his hutch, then taking off both shoes.

"I'm sure Nigella thought it was very original," Stupeedo replied, trying to put a positive spin on events. Deidre did look ever so depressed.

The Great Stupeedo's trick – the Colossal Cannon Fire act – was a guaranteed winner, or so the human cannonball thought. It involved him being fired out of a cannon and into something mightily terrifying called the Basket of Doom. From a distance, the basket appeared to be made out of dangerous, coarse barbed wire – which of course would have been rather uncomfortable to land in. But when viewed close up it was clearly made of soft and yielding satin, stiffened into peaks when needed by spray starch. There was some orange silk that, when placed near a

wind machine, looked like flames inside the basket. Clive had been instructed to make lots of pained expressions to the audience, pretending that he was scared for Stupeedo, as this made the trick far more effective. If Maureen had been around, Stupeedo would have asked for special lighting and the wind machine, but it was not to be and so he would have to cope on his own.

Stupeedo was due on in seconds. Uncle Potty had been given the task of lighting the Lithuanian touchpaper on stage, so the human cannonball had given him some advice, which actually meant Stupeedo rambling on about the nature of the job.

"Pulling a rabbit out of a hat must be a

damn sight easier than shooting yourself out of a cannon twice a week," he said. "It hurts your bottom, you know. And the explosives are getting more expensive too. The crowds keep expecting more and more. It's not enough that you shoot yourself out of the ruddy thing – the audience always want you to land on something more sharp, more prickly and more life-threatening than ever before. The honest truth is that I'd love to go back to mini-cabbing, although it can be difficult working for yourself and having people be sick on your upholstery."

Uncle Potty nodded politely, while trying to guide Stupeedo on to the stage. Uncle Potty hoped that Esmé and Monty were

getting on all right with the trunk.

Clive was working hard in Maureen's absence – he had cleared the stage, then set up the basket, wheeled in the cannon and moved the spotlight accordingly. Uncle Potty helped Stupeedo climb into the machine – which was quite tough as Lycra-clad Stupeedo had clearly been eating more pork pies recently and his middle was expanding.

Uncle Potty took a deep breath, reached for the extra-strength Lithuanian touchpaper and lit a match.

Back in the dressing room, when Maureen realised that two children – who were absolutely,

irrefutably not allowed in any part of the International Magic Guys HQ – had been put in charge of helping her escape from the trunk, it was too late for her to care. If Nigella spotted them, so be it. Monty had managed to poke a straw through one of the breathing holes and now Maureen was enjoying some lemonade, so that was something.

Esmé was concentrating on picking the lock.

"Oh, bother!" she said, frustrated. The hairclips did not seem to be doing the job.

"Do you think we'll make it in time?" Esmé asked Monty.

"I've been thinking," answered Monty. "We could hack into the trunk with a large,

mystical sword. Dr Pompkins uses one for several of his tricks."

"That might be a bit extreme," replied Esmé.

Esmé looked at the lemonade straw and it gave her an idea.

"Maureen," she addressed the trunk. "The breathing holes might be the weakest link in the whole trunk. Have you anything sharp like a penknife that I can pass through and you can make the holes bigger from the inside?"

The trunk knocked once. There was more muffled talking.

"We can't hear you, Maureen," said Monty. "Speak up".

"Oh, this is impossible!" yelled Esmé. "We'll never set Maureen Houdini free!"

At this moment Jimi walked into the dressing room with the Global Snack Tea Trolley. "Maureen, cup of tea before you go on—"

"She's stuck!" explained Esmé.

"What are you two doing here?" asked Jimi. "I thought that children were not allowed—"

"It's a long story," said Esmé. "Jimi, have you brought a knife with you, or something small that we could use to pass through to Maureen?"

"I have a slim cheese knife that might do the trick."

Jimi handed Esmé the cutlery and she leant over the trunk.

"Coming through, Maureen... Yes, it fits! Now, if you just try and enlarge some of the breathing holes, we'll have you out in no time."

Deidre appeared with her finger bleeding.

"What happened?" asked Jimi.

"Bernard," replied Deidre crossly. "I'm never giving him energy tablets again."

"I have some plasters," said Esmé, fishing out the packet in her pocket. "Meanwhile, I think Maureen has a chance of being out for the show's finale."

"And of course," yelled the Great Stupeedo

from the cannon, "I shall be entering the jaws of disaster as I leap into the Basket of Doom. Will I survive? Or will I end it all being speared on the Mighty Barb of Immediate Expiration that lies in the middle of the basket, slightly on fire?"

Here, Clive acted "scared" for Stupeedo, as instructed to do so. He pointed to a spray-starched piece of silk that poked out of the basket.

Uncle Potty solemnly lit the fuse and stood well back. The audience hushed and Stupeedo lowered his head. There was a small fizzling sound as the fuse got shorter and shorter.

Booooouuuummmmmph!

The Lithuanian touchpaper was a lot mightier than Uncle Potty had expected. It had the effect of rocketing the Great Stupeedo out of the cannon in a grand arc. Of course, he was aiming for the Basket of Doom, but Maureen usually dealt with the cannon angles and any maths stuff. Stupeedo went wildly off-course, hitting the lighting rig and bouncing back to land on an astonished Clive Pastel.

"Argh, ow!" Stupeedo got up quickly, but Clive remained curled up in a ball. "You all right, mate?" he asked.

"*Oooofgh!* Broccoli!" Clive squealed, using the IMG code word that had been devised in case anyone got into trouble on stage. "My leg hurts."

"Sorry," said Stupeedo.

"Clive!" Uncle Potty rushed over to his assistant. "Curtains, please, Deidre!"

Deidre pulled the curtain cord swiftly.

"Let's announce a quick interval," Stupeedo suggested. "Someone take Clive to hospital."

Uncle Potty stuck his head round the curtain. "Ladies and gentlemen, an interval. If you could all mingle with Nigella and say nice things about the show… er, that will be all."

He tried very hard not to look in Nigella's direction, but couldn't help noticing the one stern face in the crowd. Had the IMG messed

up the show already? Surely there was time to put on a spectacular finale. Surely.

As Uncle Potty and Deidre lifted Clive and set him on a chair in the wings, Uncle Potty was frantic. "What are we going to do? I need an assistant for my Cage of Possibilities act… someone small, speedy and keen… but where will I find such a person at this short notice?"

An excerpt from

Dr Pompkins – Totality Magic

TRICK: Dead or Alive

Dear friend of mine, Mr Alfred Burlefinger, was a great entertainer. He would supply his dinner guests with eight business cards, then request all of them to write the name of living people whom he did not know upon the cards, with the exception of one guest who was asked to write the name of a dead person on the card. The cards were then given to Burlefinger who would always discover who the dead person was.

How did he perform such a feat? What Burlefinger had done – and the spectators were never ever to guess – was give one person a hard 2H lead pencil to write the deceased person's name, when all the others had been given soft 4B pencils. Hah!

His dinner guests were always enraptured and never guessed how he did it.

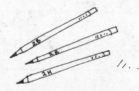

Cheating Death

Sometimes we magicians have to cheat death ourselves. Barry Houdini was said to have done this many times but was notoriously stringent in the set-up and execution of all his stunts and knew he was never really in danger. Clever chap. Once I immersed myself in perfume and ran through a display of scented candles in a Birmingham department store. But never again!

In all totality,

Dr Pompkins

CHAPTER TWELVE

The Cage of Possibilities

During the hastily arranged interval, the magicians gathered in Maureen's dressing room. They each stood around trunk number twenty-seven, staring vacantly at the intense woodiness and not-easy-to-escape-from-ness. No one had the heart to say it, but they were all thinking that the IMG was finally doomed. Clive Pastel would have been staring too, but he was sitting on a plastic chair by the back exit, waiting for his mother to turn up and drive him to the doctor's.

Stupeedo was exhausted and Deidre's finger hurt. But Uncle Potty was the most upset – he was supposed to go on next. "What on earth am I going to do?" he asked woefully. "I can't do the act without Maureen. It won't be any good – there will be no atmosphere, no lights, no dry ice, no levers and worst of all – no assistant."

"Well," said Deidre. "Perhaps there is someone who could help you out with that."

"Who?" Uncle Potty asked.

"Monty, of course," smiled Deidre.

Monty could not believe what he was hearing. An hour ago Deidre had wanted him and his sister gone. But due to the turn of events, he was now to be made magician's assistant! Monty was thrilled – it was a dream come true.

Uncle Potty thought for a moment. "It could work, I suppose. Monty knows the trick – he's seen Clive and I rehearse for hours. He's small, he's speedy... But what if Nigella sees him?"

"I'll wear the mouse costume!" pleaded Monty.

"Hm," said Uncle Potty, holding up a small furry suit. "Looks like it will fit. But it's still a gamble..."

"It's worth a try," said Monty. "I'll do the best I can."

216

"OK, but let me talk you through the trick one more time…" answered Uncle Potty.

As they were talking, Esmé looked at the breathing holes in the trunk and was sure that they had become bigger. Was the cheese knife working? Could Maureen perform her own escape?

"I'll do the lights," Deidre was telling the magicians. "Stupeedo can hide under the trap door, then take Monty's place in the box when they dim."

"Wonderful," said Uncle Potty.

"Now if Monty suddenly needs to stop the performance for whatever reason the code word is 'broccoli'," Deidre told the Pepper twins. "Esmé, you watch from the wings and if you hear 'broccoli', pull the stage curtains closed."

"OK," replied Esmé.

"The plan is almost foolproof!" said Uncle Potty, excited again. "Now let's do this!"

Nigella Spoon had enjoyed a brief chat with Jimi during the interval as he stood with the Global Snack Tea Trolley in the auditorium. She had been impressed by his array of teas and coffees, including a delicious Lapsang Souchong that had just the right balance of smokiness and tannin.

"I do like a man who knows his tea," said Nigella, brightening a little. "I asked a small man to bring me a coffee ages ago and it never showed."

"What have you made of the performances so far?" Jimi asked.

"Hm…" replied Nigella, tight-lipped.

Usually, if Nigella had wanted to close a club she would have made up her mind by this point, but she liked to wait until after the finale to give the performers a long, laboured speech telling everyone how "sorry" she was, but "needs must" and how budgets were being "squashed" and belts "tightened" and how it really would be nice if they all "stayed friends", but "with great sadness" the club was doomed and would shortly be converted into luxury flats.

There was not much hope in Nigella's

stony heart that the IMG was going to redeem itself after the two very poor performances from Deidre and Stupeedo, but Miss Spoon was a professional and was not going to let slip to anyone – even Jimi – until the final curtain descended.

A low bell sounded to draw the audience back for the start of the second half.

"Excuse me," said Nigella, leaving Jimi by the tea urn. "More magic!" she sighed, trying not to sound disappointed.

Esmé was watching nervously from the wings as Uncle Potty took to the stage. He spoke in a booming voice: "Ladies and gentlemen, we now have the Grand Finale – The Cage of

Possibilities! Can a meagre mouse turn into a brave lion?" At this point Potty was hiding his nerves well.

Monty followed Uncle Potty on to the stage on all fours, wearing the mouse costume. He stood up and as he did so Deidre swung a large spotlight on to him. The audience applauded in expectation of a great performance.

"The mouse is sleepy and so he hops into his lovely box to keep him snug," Uncle Potty announced.

Uncle Potty instructed Monty to go into the box and Monty dutifully hopped in. Monty had been so looking forward to his stage debut that he had not paused

221

to consider what being curled up in a box for more than a minute would be like – especially in a hot mouse costume. Within a few seconds, Monty was beginning to swelter.

"Ladies and gentlemen, I will put my special mousey box in a protective cage," said Uncle Potty. He lifted the box and put it on a cage with casters.

"And to make mousey feel nice and sleepy," Uncle Potty knew his lines back to front, "I will start twirling him round and round."

Here Deidre tried to dim the spotlight, but nothing happened.

Esmé watched as Uncle Potty twirled the cage round and round. She could see that without a change of lighting, and without music, or dry ice… or any sort of effect, the trick looked clunky and, well, boring. The "magic" just wasn't there. But what could they do? Maureen was out of action and that was that.

The sound of rusty castors on wooden boards was not kind on the ears. The cage lurched as it twirled and was clearly hard for Uncle Potty to control. The trick was looking less and less professional by the minute.

Esmé quickly realised what she had to do. Hoping she would be in time, Esmé ran back to Maureen and the trunk.

In Maureen's dressing room, Esmé saw

that there was a definite gap in the side of the trunk where three of the breathing holes had been.

"Maureen Houdini?" asked Esmé.

"Yes?" said the IMG leader, who for the first time in twelve hours was able to be heard through the larger gap in the trunk.

"Thank goodness!" cried Esmé with relief. "Firstly, are you all right?"

"Yes, I have studied under the great practitioners of Eastern philosophy and I have learnt to be very patient while locked in a very small box, but I must say, all this is becoming quite tiresome."

"We'll have you out soon," said Esmé. "Meanwhile, you are going to have to tell me how to operate the levers and the dry-ice machine. The International Magic Guys will be ruined if the finale continues without any technical help."

"You're telling me it's looking… not very professional?"

Esmé gulped. "Yes, I'm afraid so."

"Right then," said the trunk. "Do you have any experience of conjuring?"

"None at all."

"OK…" It was a huge decision for Maureen to start telling someone she'd only known for a few minutes about the inner workings of the International Magic Guys, but Maureen felt she had no other choice. She would give Esmé the information that no one else in the world was party to, and that information would have to save the IMG.

"See the painting of my father? Lift it up and press the red button underneath."

As Esmé moved the Picasso, then pressed the button, a section of the wall rotated to reveal a small bookshelf filled with titles such as *The Art of Deception, Now That's What I Call Magic 32, Barry Houdini's Sixty Best Harnesses* and many more.

"Pick up *The Real International Magic Guys' Floorplan*, Esmé," said Maureen. "This is where the classified stuff is. If you can decipher it, it will lead you to the brains of the operation, the technology behind the pizzazz."

Esmé took the slim floorplan from the shelf and opened it up. It was like an old treasure map – written in silver pen on parchment. There were all sorts of strange figures on it – coordinates, maybe? Clearly, the author of this plan did not want anyone to know the Houdini Secret. But was it too complicated for Esmé to work out?

Remembering that she had once taken part in a school orienteering class, that involved walking round the park trying to look for a small metal filing box filled with fruit-flavoured chews, Esmé concentrated hard on the symbols and numbers. Soon, they started to make sense – and if she understood the map correctly, which she thought she did, the technical wizardry was located in the wings! So it had been under the IMG members' noses all along...

Esmé Pepper was the only person in the building who had the reasoning to work out where the place that housed the all-important levers was.

"Go, Esmé! Make the magic happen," said Maureen. "I'll be out of here soon.

"And remember," she added. "If you need some *oomph*, press the 'Houdini' button."

Clutching the diagram, Esmé ran to the wings. The map pointed to a curtain, which looked like an ordinary velvet curtain, but when she pulled it back there was a large wardrobe behind it, with a small sign that read "Operations". Esmé tried to turn the handle, but it was stiff. She rattled it again, and the door flew open to reveal a high-tech bank of knobs and buttons, levers and pulleys. Some were marked, others were not. There was a small bank of lights that were constantly flashing on and off, in random sequence. It looked like the flight deck of a science-fiction spaceship, if that spaceship was actually a wardrobe and right in the centre of the console was a bright red button marked "Houdini".

Esmé glanced round – she could see everyone on stage from this angle. Whether Uncle Potty could see her she did not know, as he was too busy twirling the cage round and round to notice more than what was in front of his one eyebrow.

Esmé looked at the map again, but there was no clue as to which button to press first.

I just have to press one... Whatever it might do, thought Esmé, who somehow had more confidence than she had imagined before.

Esmé spotted a button marked "anti-gravity", pressed it and waited to see what would happen.

An excerpt from

Dr Pompkins – Totality Magic

TRICK: The Vanishing Pencil

A pencil is rolled in a sheet of paper. The magician quickly tears the paper to pieces, and the pencil is gone... How do you do it?

The pencil is just a hollow paper tube. Make the tube out of coloured paper and in one end insert a real pencil tip and an eraser in the other.

As you can write something florid and elegant with the pencil before you wrap it up, it will seem nothing out of the ordinary.

But when you roll it up in a sheet of paper, you can tear the paper easily and prove that the pencil has vanished.

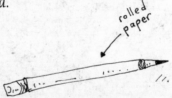

rolled paper

Customised Clothing

When I am rifling through my suit jacket, trying to find such a pencil or a small flask of whisky, I am alarmed at how many pockets Mrs Dr Pompkins has sewn into my linings. Pockets are a must, if you are to make things appear out of "thin air" – flowers, extra wands, pencils, cats, ladders and such like. The trick is that they must be easy to get to. All your stage clothing must be adaptable.

Dr Pompkins

CHAPTER THIRTEEN

A Mouse, a Lion and One Hundred Doves

Montague Pepper was rather itchy inside the box, but at least the itchiness was taking his mind off feeling hot and at least the heat was taking his mind off the cramp in his left foot. Uncle Potty continued to twirl the cage faster and faster, while waiting for Stupeedo to knock lightly on the top of the trap door. This would let Uncle Potty know he could stop twirling, release the bottom of the cage and Stupeedo would be ready to catch "mousey".

Inside the box, Monty tried to look on the bright side: if he was going to become a magician, he would have to get used to feeling hot and itchy. This was his apprenticeship.

Uncle Potty had been twirling the cage around for over five whole minutes and the audience were becoming bored. Some of them checked their phones for messages and many were dozing off. Nigella and the panel from the PCMC were almost completely uninterested by now, realising the International Magic Guys could not make the grade.

"Yentovitz, the Club Eviction papers, please. And a pen," whispered Nigella.

Nigella took the forms and started to fill them out.

On stage, Monty was still feeling sick. "Uncle Potty," he called. "Just slow down!"

But Uncle Potty did not hear. He was informing the audience as part of the routine about how mice "sleep for over fourteen hours a day" and "never even wake up for a glass of water" or "a burp".

Monty didn't want to shout "broccoli" – he knew that he shouldn't stop the show, but the twirling was insufferable. He had to shout "broccoli". Now. For all he was worth.

But just as he was about to yell, Monty felt

the box lift and rise into the air. How had this happened?

Esmé had a quick look round the curtain at the stage to see the cage smoothly ascend. This was more like it! But where was the atmosphere? Esmé pressed a button marked "mood music" and at once a lilting piano sonata wafted through the speakers. The "dry ice" button also provided a theatrical fog to the proceedings. Pretty soon Esmé had mastered the small bank of controls that operated the lights, and dimmed them, then added a green tinge to the stage. This was fun. With another button, glitter descended from the ceiling and caught the lights like magic, green snow. Esmé felt her heart beat fast and was thrilled to see the effects were making the show look absolutely spectacular.

"What are you doing?" Deidre joined Esmé in the wings, having left the old manual spotlight when she noticed the cage levitate and the dry ice appear. "What are these buttons and levers?"

"Maureen gave me the map," whispered Esmé. "I worked out where the levers were kept – behind a wardrobe door."

"So this is the Operations room!" It had taken Deidre a while to realise. "My goodness, Esmé, you've found it! I've been a member of the IMG for thirty years and never figured out where it was. The Houdini

secret! It's yours!"

Esmé smiled. She gazed out into the audience, where formerly uninterested people were now beginning to smile. Yentovitz had starting paying attention – even Nigella, who had been busy completing the Club Eviction form, looked up in surprise. The cage was flying, there was music... *OK. Maybe this is good*, Nigella thought. *At least it's better than it was...*

With the cage high in the air, Esmé decided to crank another lever, which made the trap door open. Stupeedo, dressed as a lion, suddenly rose up on to stage level.

The audience gasped. This was something unexpected! From the wings Deidre Lemons gazed at the stage in awe. This was fantastic. Deidre felt a ripple of "old times" down her shoulders, a whisper of "halcyon days" by her neck and a gargle of "yesteryear's laughter" in her throat. Her tiara caught the light and shone. Her teeth, which had been whitened on the cheap two years ago, glimmered slightly. Danger. Excitement. Levitation.

But for Stupeedo, the unexpected was not a good thing. He was meant to replace Monty inside the box, but Monty was now many metres above the stage. The Great Stupeedo simply did not know what to do. He stared at Uncle Potty in bewilderment.

"My my!" said Uncle Potty, improvising. "Look how the Cage Of Possibilities travels out of sight of the great lion!"

The lion shrugged.

Esmé snuck a look at the stage and saw the confusion. "What do I do now?" she whispered to Deidre. "Stupeedo wouldn't even fit in the box if he tried, he's far too big."

Esmé pressed another button and the cage lowered back down. A large puff of dry ice squirted at Stupeedo, the music changed to a crazy violin solo and the sequins turned to balloons.

The audience howled with laughter. What would happen next?

Monty needed to get out of the box, he felt truly ill and his legs ached. Maybe he had gone through the trap door and was under the stage by now – although he could have been in Swindon he felt so disorientated.

For the moment, Uncle Potty was having to provide an entertaining front as best he could.

"As you can see, my lovely guests, the lion has roared!" He looked at Stupeedo, hoping that he would roar.

"Roar," said Stupeedo, still bewildered.

"What will poor mousey do now? Confront the beast?" Uncle Potty did not know what mousey would do, or what mousey should do. He did not really know what anyone was doing, but he was really enjoying himself.

Esmé saw the chaos and realised that there

242

was only one thing for it: The "Houdini" button. She located it and pressed it once firmly.

As Monty stood up and dizzily stepped out of the box on to the stage, he accidentally knocked Stupeedo back down the trap door. At once, fireworks went off at the back of the stage and the rear curtain fell to reveal a huge neon sign that read "International Magic Guys". A hundred doves appeared from the curtain.

"The angry lion becomes a hundred peaceful doves," Uncle Potty told the rapt audience, as he lifted his foot and placed it lightly on Stupeedo's head, which was sticking out of the trap door. Esmé watched as Monty tried to flap the birds away – this was utter mayhem, but to the audience it looked like Monty was conducting events. Most of the birds landed on the cage, which then rose high into the air again, where they started pecking at each other.

"The mouse wins against the lion! All hail mousey!" said Uncle Potty, who was still loving every minute. A firework exploded again and rained a thousand sequins.

The audience lapped this up. They were wild for fireworks, the neon sign, the doves – and they especially loved "mousey". Stupeedo's helmeted head sticking out of the trap door was just hilarious. Nigella was pleased – now this *was* a finale. A good one.

Maybe the IMG deserved a second chance. Maybe the IMG was actually a good magic club.

But Monty could take no more. He was too hot and felt sick. He reached up and took the mouse head off and stood blinking in the brightness of the spotlights.

Nigella's face turned from rosy and delighted to bright white and not-very-pleased-at-all.

"There is a *child* in this building!" Nigella shouted, as if she'd seen a mouse – which was ironic, as Monty was dressed as one.

"This is against the rules!" she barked. "Let me speak to Maureen Houdini. The IMG is finished!"

Silence descended. Every single person knew that children were not allowed in the IMG building. Nigella was furious; she felt that she and the PCMC had been made fools of.

Esmé was horrified – they had been so close to success, even with the glitches in the finale. Something needed to be done and she would not let Nigella close the IMG.

Esmé spotted the dairy creamer tubs on Jimi's tea trolley in the wings. Hadn't Monty mentioned he had a favourite trick – the Dairy Creamer Eye Splurge?

Esmé cupped her hands round her mouth and shouted "broccoli!" at her twin.

Monty looked over at his sister and

wondered if she was in trouble. Why was she waving something at him? It looked like… yes, it was… a tub of Dairy Creamer. All at once Monty realised what Esmé wanted him to do. He smiled and nodded at his twin. Just as Nigella was opening her mouth to start shouting at everyone, Esmé threw something to Monty who quickly hid it, then turned and faced the audience.

"Wait!" he commanded. "I have the trick of all tricks to perform."

Uncle Potty, Deidre and Stupeedo took a step away from Monty as Esmé dimmed the lights and centred a clean white spotlight on her twin.

Monty was a little apprehensive as he

cupped the creamer in his left hand behind his back, but he breathed in deeply and started the routine.

First, he instructed the audience to watch closely. "I promise you, that if each of you remain silent after this trick, I will give every one of you fifty pounds."

Esmé was intrigued. Monty didn't have a single fifty-pound note that he could hand out to the hundred or so members of the IMG. She recalled that he had about two pounds in his savings box at home, which he was keeping for "magical emergencies". *Monty must be certain that this trick will work,* she thought.

Montague Pepper was indeed becoming

more assured. "And if you don't stay silent, you will each pay me ten pounds."

The audience smiled silently. Of course they could stay quiet! They had seen plenty of magic tricks and they were each confident that nothing would faze them during Monty's performance.

Monty smiled. He had concealed the small carton in his left hand and counted slowly to ten in his head, a pause that he hoped would increase the tension within the audience. Steadily and dramatically, he brought his left hand up to his brow, and along with it the hidden carton of dairy creamer.

"Woe is me!" he cried. "For I am at war with myself!"

Esmé hoped that being in the box hadn't had a bad effect on her brother. Was he actually ill? He still looked a bit sweaty. Esmé wondered if she should have brought a thermometer and first-aid kit with her, along with the plasters.

"Aaargh!" continued Monty, making a gargling sound with his throat. The boy seemed monstrously, but mysteriously unwell. "I cannot see, my right eye has been blighted by the fear of the Pan-Continental Magic Corporation."

The audience laughed, while Nigella Spoon turned to her colleagues stiffly. What did the boy mean? Did he have a history of emotional "episodes"? But if Montague was feeling peaky, this was part of the act. With the milk carton concealed over his left eye he swiftly brought his right hand up to his face and shouted,

"Damn you, eye! Time to gouge thee out!" Monty poked his index finger into the creamer, his supposed eye. Creamy white "mucus" shot everywhere – on to his shoes, the stage and some of the audience.

"Ooouuuuwww!" Everyone in the hall yelled – some in sympathy, others in horror, genuinely believing the deranged child had poked his eye out. No one, as Monty predicted, could help but shout. None stayed silent, none at all.

Monty held out the empty creamer cup.

"That, my friends, is magic," he announced and smiled.

The formerly horrified members of the audience each stood up in their seats and applauded. What a marvellous trick! What an amazing child!

But Esmé was keen to see Nigella's reaction. What would she make of this? Did the IMG have a chance?

The magicians clapped and whooped, pulling money out of their wallets and giving the rolls of banknotes to a stunned Monty. Some were still unsure he was all right, and were trying to call NHS Direct on their mobiles. Monty was astonished the trick had actually worked, and over the moon that he had succeeded. As more crinkly notes were stuffed in his pockets, Nigella Spoon stood up and walked towards the stage.

Monty stood frozen. Nigella's face was stern and he feared the worst.

But the grimace turned into a grin as Nigella walked on to the stage itself.

"What a fantastic trick! Young man, you are a credit to the world of magic. You have outwitted everyone here."

"Thank you," said Monty. "I tried my best."

"But you know that we do have a policy about children."

Uncle Potty stood forward. "We have known this all along," he explained. "But

you do not know just how much the children have helped today."

"Children?" asked Nigella. "Are there more?"

Esmé took this as her cue to appear from the wings. Nigella was shocked to see another child in the building, but she was thinking fast. She turned to Yentovitz. "Remind me of the exact wording, please."

Yentovitz consulted his electronic device and read from it: "Clause fifty-one, section b) of the Juvenile Ruling Act means that no child is allowed in any of the Pan-Continental Magic Corporation clubs in a professional or junior capacity. And that is final."

"What if we join the dots, Yentovitz?"

asked Nigella. "Would you check the stats on all our clubs in Britain, please? Are they doing well, as a whole?"

Yentovitz started tapping at the device. After a few minutes he replied, "No, not really."

"And do you think that has something to do with the fact that we tell our clubs not to admit children?"

Yentovitz looked blank. He wasn't accustomed to having his own opinion. Uncle Potty started grinning from ear to ear.

"Perhaps you need to reverse this policy straight away," Esmé told Nigella politely.

"You took the words right out of my mouth," replied Miss Spoon.

"OK. Let's do it. Children are now welcome!"

"In all totality!" added a freed Maureen, emerging from the wings.

Dr Pompkins – Totality Magic Thank You...

Thank you for accompanying me on our Dr Pompkins – Totality Magic journey; we are almost at the destination: success. I hope that I have given you a glimpse of the magician's world, so close that some of you have smelt the oily collar of some of the finest magicians past and present. I don't need to give you a trick – you now know all the basics. Hurrah!

In all totality,

Dr Pompkins

CHAPTER FOURTEEN

A Magnificent Day

Everyone looked round, stunned, as Maureen nonchalantly walked on to centre stage.

The IMG members in the auditorium applauded – not knowing she had been stuck in a trunk all this time. Although if they had known she had been stuck in a trunk they would have clapped louder. Each audience member wore a Maureen Houdini button badge. Maureen was delighted to see her own smiling face beaming up from so many velvet lapels.

"Nigella Spoon," she said, greeting her adversary with an outstretched hand. "So nice to see you."

"What took you so long?" Nigella shook Maureen's hand firmly.

"Just having a lie-in," explained Maureen. "Did I hear you say you are going to allow children into the International Magic Guys? Good job too. Some would say that the place was getting a bit stale."

Uncle Potty, Deidre and Stupeedo were a bit ruffled by this comment, but each decided not to say anything.

"I propose that we start an International Magic Guys Junior Division and roll the idea out to the rest of the country in the next few days," Nigella told Maureen, attempting a broad grin, which only made her look as if she had eaten a very bony, very fishy fish.

"And the first member..." Yentovitz pointed to Monty.

"...Is Montague Pepper," prompted Esmé. Then, to her brother: "The Eye Splurge really is a great trick."

"I think we have many things to discuss," Nigella told Maureen. "Did you see much of the show, by the way...?"

"Well, no, I didn't," answered Maureen.

As the ladies started talking, Esmé

whispered to her brother. "How did Maureen get out?"

"I have no idea," came Monty's reply. "Magic?"

"Cup of tea, anyone? Light scone, petit fours or maybe a piece of baklava?" Jimi pulled the Global Snack Tea Trolley on to the stage. Soon everyone was enjoying a delicious bite to eat and marvelling at the thought of a new IMG Junior Division. New talent. Fresh ideas.

Uncle Potty patted Monty on the back. "Excellent trick, something special. How much money did you make?"

Monty looked in his pockets. They were stuffed with rolls of notes all given to him by the delighted audience.

"Maybe we could build some kind of club house for the IMG kids," Monty said to Esmé, while enjoying a scone. "And I'll get you a new watch."

"You could also do with some new chairs," added Gladstone, who was on his third baklava.

"I might even put some aside for a new tweed cape for you, Uncle Potty," laughed Monty. "One that doesn't smell of mackerel."

Uncle Potty was delighted by the way things had turned out.

"This has been a magnificent day, in all totality!" he told the Pepper children. "Thank you, Esmé and Monty, for saving our club."

"Oh, it wasn't just us," said Esmé. "Everyone helped out, didn't they?"

Esmé smiled at Monty; she was so proud of him.

Maureen Houdini finished her chat with Nigella and approached Esmé.

"How did you get out of the trunk in the end?" asked Esmé, who wasn't a fan of the unexplained.

"I think the cheese knife had something to do with it," Maureen said with a wink. "I've been thinking that the new Junior Division could do with someone with strong technical skills to help them out backstage. Interested?"

Esmé beamed proudly. She had been

sceptical about magic to begin with, but now she could see it involved a lot of skill and even more fun. "Count me in," she replied. "I'd be honoured to help."

Monty ran up to his twin, joyfully. "I've just signed some autographs! Today has been incredible. Esmé, it's been the best day of my life."

Esmé grinned and hugged her brother. "In all totality," she said.

Afterword by Dr Pompkins

And thus we have seen how the world of magic turns ordinary life into one filled with wonder – magic is here to entertain, to delight, to surprise. Be the best you can be, dear reader, keep learning, keep performing - keep the spirit alive! And remember to keep a currant bun in one of your many pockets in case you are caught hungry "on the hoof".

Yours,

Dr Pompkins

Relaxing with a small glass of sherry, South of France

THE PEPPERS

AND THE ISLAND OF INVENTION

Join the Pepper twins on their next fantastic
adventure full of magic and mayhem!

Esmé, Monty and their Uncle Potty have
been summoned to the Sea Spray Theatre
on the end of Crab Pie Pier. They're on a
mission to keep the old theatre from closing
and must perform the show of a lifetime to
reel in the crowds.

But not everyone wants the theatre to survive
and a certain someone is determined to
sabotage the show, whatever the cost...

Add a strange island hideaway full of zany
inventions, a hair-raising helicopter rescue-
mission and the world's biggest goldfish
bowl and the Peppers are in for an
unforgettable summer!

Coming soon!

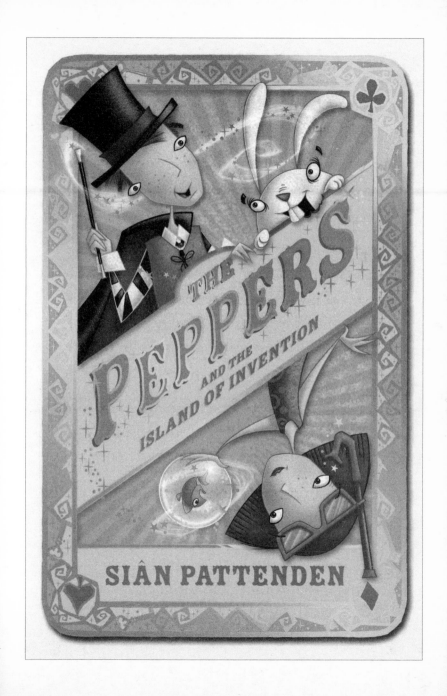